A BONFIRE
IN THE
SKY

This book is for Ralph Eady,
fellow pilot, and longtime friend
who has shared so many
of my campfires
and gone so many
hundreds of miles with me
through the mountains and deserts
of Arizona.

A BONFIRE IN THE SKY

A Novel
by
John Kosek

REGENT PRESS
2000

ISBN: 1-889059-80-3

Manufactured in the United States of America
REGENT PRESS
6020-A Adeline
Oakland, CA 94608

*My special thanks for help
in the preparation of this book
go to Aviation Historian Ralph Eady
and to the Luke family,
especially Frank's niece, Helen Sherry McCall
who saved all the newspaper
articles and Frank's sister,
Eva Luke Flyn
who so generously shared
her memories of Frank with me
over the years.*

Table of Contents

Although this is a work of fiction, it incorporates the names of real places and real people and actual events. World War I, after all, did happen. No offense is intended in the portrayal of any organization or individual. Some of the participants, I realize, might like to speak to amend or correct some aspects of this tale.

None are alive to do so. Even if they were alive, could they accurately remember what was said and done after all these years? And if they could remember, would they tell the truth no matter how painful or self deprecating it might be? It somehow seems unlikely.

This, then, in the absence of any better account, is the way it was.

July 22nd, 1918

27th Pursuit Squadron

Saints Airfield

Chateau Thiery

France

Chapter 1

The Model T touring car, the headlights only dim yellow glows in the dark, splashed through the muddy, rutted road and drew to a stop in front of the officer's mess. The driver and his passenger had to half shout to make themselves heard above the drumming of the rain on the canvas top and the isinglass side curtains.

"There's lights in the mess," the driver said. "You should be able to find someone there to report to. I'll take your things over to the officers quarters. Then, with your permission sir, I'll be on my way back to headquarters. These roads will be axle deep if it keeps up like this much longer."

"Fine," the officer reached over and shook the driver's hand. "Good luck on the trip back, corporal."

"And good luck to you sir."

The officer pulled his raincoat tightly around him and opened the car door. A long jump carried him to a board sidewalk and then he was up the steps of the mess and at the door. The throttle was advanced on the Model T, the low pedal pushed to the floor and the hand clutch engaged. It crawled around the circular drive and stopped in front of a long low barracks.

The officer, a 2nd Lieutenant, opened the door of the mess and found himself in an entryway with raincoats hung along both walls. He took off his own coat and shook the water off and hung it on an empty hook. Behind a doorway to his left he could hear the sound of music and from time to time some loud laughing. He took off his service cap and ran his hand through his hair to straighten it.

Opening the door he stepped into a rather large, smoke filled room. There was a bar to his right and tables and chairs to his left

There were probably two dozen men there, all officers except for the bartender. Many of the men seemed to be quite drunk. None of them seemed to take any particular notice of him. He looked around for the gold leaves of a major, but saw no one with a rank higher than a Captain and that man wore the insignia of a medical officer.

One of the men sitting on the bar had an accordion and he was trying to get his fingers set right on the keys. One of the others was trying to help him. There were a few false starts and then he and a half dozen of the others at the bar launched out on the chorus of a song that by tradition could only be sung by pursuit pilots on combat assignments at the front.

"Now stand to your glasses, steady!
The world is a world of lies:
A cup for the dead already,
And here's to the next man that dies."

The Captain had noticed him by the door and had come over to where he stood during the singing. "Can I help you Lieutenant?"

"I'm Lieutenant Luke, Frank Luke, reporting for duty with the 27th Pursuit Squadron. I have my orders right here sir."

The man reached out and shook his hand. "Captain Holden, I'm the squadron surgeon. You can forget your orders for now. Major Hartney and Captain Grant have gone off to a meeting at group headquarters. We'll get you checked in the morning. But come on and I'll introduce you to some of the other pilots."

They worked their way along the bar and the Captain made the introductions. They stopped at the group at the end that had been singing. "Have a drink with us Lieutenant," they offered.

He hesitated, "Well a beer maybe."

The bartender served him up a large schooner.

"So where are you from Frank? It is Frank isn't it?"

"Yes, I'm from Phoenix, that's in Arizona."

"You got the Indians all under control out there now?"

"Oh sure, they all put on clothes now when they come into town."

"Put on clothes. You mean they used to come into town naked?"

"They did, until the ladies in the town put a stop to it."

"Exactly how did they do that?"

"Well, on the road to the reservation, there's a big mesquite tree just outside of town and the ladies went and hung all kinds of old clothes on it, men's, women's, children's. Now when the Indians come into town they have to stop at the tree and find some clothes that fit them and put them on. Then when they leave town they hang the clothes back up on the tree so that some other Indians can use them."

They laughed all around at that. "Do you expect us to believe that?"

"You can if you want to."

They laughed again. "What's your school, Frank?"

"School?"

"Where did you go to school?"

"Phoenix Union."

"Phoenix Union," the one laughed. "Is that some kind of Reform School?"

"No, it's the high school in town."

"High school!" They all laughed again. "Boys, he's a high school graduate. Imagine that."

"Come on, lay off," one of them said.

No one said anything and Luke sipped at his beer. If he had taken any offense at what was said, he gave no sign of it. Except for the rain rattling on the metal roof the room was suddenly quite.

Luke set his mug down on the bar. "Which ones of you are aces?" he asked.

The room was even quieter. No one said a word.

"Surely some of you are aces?"

"There's no one in here an ace," someone said in a flat voice.

"But surely some of you..."

"Our only ace went West two days ago," the same flat voice answered.

Behind Luke, one of the men nudged another and whispered, "Get O'Donnel over here and have him take this hick down a notch or two."

"How long have you been here at the front?" Luke asked.

"Long enough to know that you'll be lucky to be alive a month from now. This isn't Issoudun. The Fokkers up here shoot back and with real bullets."

"I assume that we get to use real bullets too," Luke answered. "I didn't come all this way just to let some Hennie use me for target practice."

Behind Luke, several of the pilots shook their heads. "Seems like we've heard that kind of talk before," the one said. "As I remember, the poor fellow didn't last out the week."

A tall, heavy set man came over to the group. "Welcome to the 27th," he said reaching out a big hand toward Luke. His other hand bumped against Luke's shoulder and the glass of beer in it slopped on to Luke's sleeve. "Oh, sorry," he said. "I'm Patrick O'Donnel."

He took Luke's hand and shook it and as he did he seemed to loose his balance and his beer spilled again, this time on Luke's pant leg and shoe. "Oh, sorry again there," he said. "You must think I'm awfully clumsy. Actually, I'm not. Here, I'll buy you a beer to make amends. Bartender, two beers for my friend and me here."

Behind Luke's back there were a number of sly grins.

"Are you sure that you haven't had enough to drink," Luke said letting go of the big man's hand and stepping away from him.

"What, you don't want to drink with me?" The big man, O'Donnel, acted as if he were hurt by Luke's answer.

"If I want to get soaked, I can go outside," Luke said.

"Oh, no," O'Donnel said. "You don't want to get soaked, not until you've got smashed. Then you won't notice if you get soaked. Bartender, bring those beers for my friend and me so that we can have a drink. And while you're at it I'll just go and drain my radiator." He shuffled off toward the toilet door at the end of the room.

"Don't offend him," one of the men said to Luke.

"He doesn't like to be crossed, "another cautioned him.

"He could stand to learn some manners," Luke said.

"Don't you try to teach him," the first man said. "He can be mean sometimes when he's been drinking."

"He's the heavyweight champion of New York state," the other said. "Before the war he was one of Jack Dempsy's sparring partners."

Luke looked around uncomfortably. The attention of everyone in the club seemed to be directed toward him. O'Donnel came back from the toilet.

There were two full schooners of beer on the bar and O'Donnel picked them up. He reached out to hand one to Luke and, in the process, bumped Luke's hand and spilled beer on his wrist and the cuff of his coat.

Luke held the schooner of beer for only a fraction of a second and then let it slip through his fingers and fall to the floor. It bounced and splashed beer all over O'Donnel's trousers and shoes.

"Hey, that got all over me," O'Donnel protested.

Luke had already turned his back and started to walk away. O'Donnel stepped up behind him and put his hand on his shoulder. "Mister, don't you walk away from me when I'm talking to you." He started to pull on Luke's shoulder.

Luke suddenly spun around and caught O'Donnel flush on the chin with a straight right hand that sent him staggering back across the room. Chairs and tables went over and O'Donnel hit the wall with a crash that rattled the windows. He hung there for a moment and then slowly slid down the wall and sat on the floor.

Luke was right behind him, fists doubled up and the right hand cocked and ready. A half dozen hands reached out to stop him and he shook them off the way a grizzly bear might shake off a pack of hounds. "The next man that touches me gets his arm broke," Luke warned them.

The crowd hung back away from him. The flash of violence had come so suddenly that they were all caught off guard. Those that had had their hands on him had felt the power of a barrel chest and a pair of club like arms.

"Get up!" Luke commanded the dazed O'Donnel.

"Why did you do that?" O'Donnel protested. "I didn't do anything to you. I didn't mean any harm."

"Get up!"

Tears ran down O'Donnel's cheeks. "I didn't mean any harm."

"I think you've made your point, Lieutenant." The Captain stepped between Luke and O'Donnel who remained sitting on the floor, now quietly sobbing.

"This might be a good time to get you settled in over at the barracks." The speaker was a tall dark haired Lieutenant who had been sitting alone at one of the tables. "I'll walk over with you and show you around." The tension seemed to slowly ease out of Luke and he straightened up and unclenched his fists. The tall Lieutenant led the way into the entry hall and they got their raincoats and went out into the night.

Chapter 2

☆ ☆ ☆

The room was small with beds and chests along the walls and there was a window with a chair under it. They sat on the beds across from one another. The tall, dark-haired Lieutenant reached across between the beds to shake hands and said simply, "I'm Joe Wehner."

"Frank Luke. Thanks for taking me out of there. I don't think that I was making too good an impression."

"You made a hell of an impression on me," Wehner said. "I never thought I'd see the day that someone would call O'Donnel's bluff."

"Bluff?"

"You didn't think that he was the heavyweight champion of New York?"

"He isn't?"

"It's an act," Wehner laughed. "He pulls it on all the new pilots."

"Then I was out of line." Luke said looking somewhat troubled. "I hope that he'll accept my apology,"

"He'll come and apologize to you," Wehner said. "He's not a bad sort. It's the others that egg him on and he does it to please them. But the hell with them, lets have a drink and you can tell me how you're going to be our next ace." Wehner brought a bottle of bourbon and a couple of glasses out of one of the dresser drawers.

"Oh, I don't know."

"Might as well," Wehner said, pouring some whiskey into each glass. "We've already been given the order to stand down for tomorrow. This rain stretches all the way back to Ireland."

"I know," Luke said. "I was supposed to bring a Spad from Orley, but then when the weather went sour they had me come on the train."

"How much time have you got on the Spad?" Wehner asked.

"Almost fifty hours."

"How'd you get so much?"

"I've been ferrying airplanes from the factory to the front for over a month," Luke said. "I thought I'd never get into the war."

"Well, you're into now." Wehner handed Luke one of the glasses. "Here's to your great success at the front."

The both raised their glasses and drank. But I've got to tell you," Wehner went on. "You've come to a bad squadron at a bad time."

"How so?"

"We've lost six pilots already this month, four on one patrol, the day before yesterday."

"All killed?"

"Four are dead. One is in a German hospital with his left arm amputated, the other is in a German prisoner of war camp."

"But four on one patrol," Luke said. "What happened?"

Wehner took a big drink of bourbon before he started his story. "There were eight of us," he finally said. "Escorting a two-seater taking pictures of the road running north from Chateau Thierry. We went all the way to the bridge over the River Ourcq, which was farther over the lines than I had ever been. The two seater was at eight thousand feet and four of us were five hundred feet above him and the other four were up another five hundred feet and off to one side. We were just turning to follow the two seater east along the river when, all of a sudden, there was a whole line of Fokkers, maybe as many as a dozen, bearing down on us from the north.

"Captain Grant was leading and he fired a flare to alert the two-seater and all the rest of our flight. Then he turned tail and dove back toward our lines."

"Left the two-seater, just like that?" Luke asked.

Wehner nodded. "Panicked and ran."

"And the rest of you?"

"Well," Wehner said. "That's where it gets confusing. Grant says that there were twelve of them and the only chance we had was to dive for our own lines. The way I see it the Fokkers were level with us, but McArthur, he was leading the high flight, had five hundred feet on them. If we had turned to meet their attack, he could have used his height advantage to drop down on them when he saw what their response was. It isn't as if they were all beginners up there in the high flight. McArthur had seven victories and Norton had two. We could have at least made one pass at the Fokkers and given the two-seater a couple of minutes head start back to our lines. If we didn't expect to protect the two-seater, what the hell was the use of our escorting him over the lines?

"So what happened?"

"We started our diving turn to the south," Wehner said with a cheerless look on his face. "The two seater turned south too, and also McArthur with the high flight. We were gradually pulling away from the Fokkers; the Fokker might be a little faster in level flight, but the Spad will out dive it any day. The two seater was falling behind though and two Fokkers split off to go after it. McArthur went after them and four more Fokkers split off to go after him."

"And you didn't go to help him?"

"I started to," Wehner hung his head. "But I was on the right hand side of the formation. To get to McArthur and the two seater I would have had to cross directly behind the rest of my flight and right in front of the six Fokkers that were following us. I would have never made it to him and I would have left our flight one plane short. If I could have done anything to help, I would have. McArthur was about the only friend I had in this outfit."

They sat quietly and sipped at the whisky. Outside the rain was a steady drumming against the roof and the window. Finally Wehner went on. "The last time I looked back, the two seater was burning and McArthur and the others were going around with the Fokkers. I don't know what happened after that. We heard from the Red Cross this afternoon that the men in the two seater and McArthur and Norton and Gunn were killed and that Miller had crashed and was in the hospital with his left arm amputated above the elbow. My guess is that McArthur got one or two before he went down, but I suppose that we will never know unless Miller can tell us after the war is over."

Wehner paused again to pour himself another drink and then went on bitterly, "It wouldn't have had to turn out that way. If we had attacked instead of running we might have turned the tables on them. It couldn't have turned out any worse than it did. But Grant is so goddamned afraid of Udet that he won't attack even when he has a two to one advantage on our side of the lines."

"Udet? Ernst Udet is in this part of the line?"

Wehner nodded. "He's in command of Jagstaffel 4, operating out of a couple of fields north of Chateau Thierry. We know for a fact that he personally shot down our Lieutenant Martin two weeks ago for his 56th victory. I wouldn't be surprised if he was in one of the Fokkers two days ago. Big formations are his style. You don't see a Fokker for days on end and then, all of a sudden, the sky is full of them."

Wehner reached over with the bottle to refill Luke's glass. Luke shook his head. "Not a drinker Frank?" Wehner asked.

"Not really."

"Give us some time, we'll teach you. A month or two in this squadron would make a drunk out of Billy Sunday."

Luke shrugged. "So what happened to the rest of you?"

"Oh yes, I haven't finished have I." Wehner poured himself another drink. "We kept on diving for home and the six Fokkers kept following although they were slowly falling behind us. At about three thousand feet there were some broken clouds. As deep in enemy territory as we were, we should have stayed above them, but Grant must have been afraid that if we leveled off the Fokkers would start to catch us. We went right down through a hole and there were four more Fokkers between us and our lines. We had to make a fight of it then. Elliot's fuel tank was hit on their first pass and he lost all his air pressure. Somehow he managed to slip clear of the fight and he got his engine to run on the emergency tank long enough to make a landing just over our lines. Grant would have got it too if I hadn't shot a Fokker right off his tail."

"Once they made us turn, the six behind us caught up and then it was every man for himself. We kept diving for our lines and they kept trying to cut us off. Before long we were right in the tree tops and being shot at from the ground as well as the air. Somehow I got another in a head on pass and then, miracle of all miracles, we were across their lines. Martin's engine had been hit and he made a crash landing in no-man's-land. Grant and I were the only ones who were able to make it back here. Frank, you should have seen my plane. From the cockpit back, the fabric was shredded like it had been left out in a hail storm."

"But you got two of them!"

"Yes," Wehner acknowledged. "But I only got credit for the second. The first fell so far behind the German lines that it wasn't confirmed."

"But you got him for sure?"

"I was only twenty feet behind him and I saw the bullet hit the pilot square in the back of the head."

"And Grant didn't see this happen?"

"He was so terrified that he didn't see anything. It wouldn't have mattered if he had. We can't confirm victories for each other, If they fall on the German side of the lines, they have to be verified by someone on the ground or in one of our observation balloons."

"What did your Squadron Commander, Major Hartney, say about all of this?" Luke asked.

"What could he say? Grant told his story first. He put the blame on McArthur for leaving the formation. If I had said we shouldn't have run, it would have been my word against his. But Hartney didn't like it. The pictures were important enough that they flew the mission again, only the second time they got the 94th to provide the escort. Rickenbacker himself led it."

"And what happened?"

"They never saw a single German plane."

"Hartney?" Luke wanted to know. "What's he like."

"The best," Wehner said. "He's a Canadian, been in the war almost from the start. Spent a year in the trenches and then almost two in the air service. He crashed in no-man's-land and busted up his legs and they sent him back to Canada. Somehow he got involved in training the 27th there and he's been with it ever since. He was an ace before he crashed and he's had another victory with the 27th."

"So what's the problem? What makes the 27th such a bad squadron?"

"The problem is," Wehner said. "That Hartney is leaving to take command of the whole fighter group. Grant is to be the new Squadron Commander. Without Hartney, I'm afraid that there are going to be more days like the day before yesterday. We need somebody like Rickenbacker to set an example and put a little heart into the outfit. Grant, and too many of the others, can only think about keeping themselves alive. That's what gets people killed."

There was a knock on the door. Wehner got up and opened it. It was the barracks orderly. "Sir," he said. "I was looking for Lieutenant Luke. I go off duty in a few minutes and I was wondering if he knew where he wanted his things put."

Wehner turned around. "You're welcome to bunk in here if you want, Frank. Though, God knows, we have enough empty beds right now for you to room somewhere else if you want."

"No, here is fine."

"Bring Lieutenant Luke's things than, if you will," Wehner said. The corporal went off to get them.

"We might as well bunk together," Wehner said. "Being as we're the two outcasts in the squadron."

"Outcasts?"

"You don't think that you made a lot of friends back there in the mess, do you?"

"I would hope that when I've set things right, the fight and all could be forgotten."

"Oh, that will, at least by O'Donnel. But what you said about their not being aces, that didn't go down very well. They didn't much like being reminded of their lack of success, especially by a newcomer that has yet to fly his first combat patrol."

"I see," Luke said. "I guess I did sort of talk without thinking. I should have known better." He was silent and thoughtful for a moment. "But why should you be an outcast? What have you done?"

"That's the irony of if," Wehner said. "I haven't done anything. It's because of my father."

"Father?"

"My father was born in Germany."

"Why so was mine," Luke said. "I wouldn't let anybody hold that against me."

"There's more," Wehner said.

The orderly knocked and then opened the door and put Luke's things inside. Luke set one of the cases up on the bed and opened it up.

"You should hear the rest of this before you unpack," Wehner said. "No one has wanted to live with me since before we left the states."

Luke looked at him questioningly and Wehner went on. "I speak German fluently, I can read a German newspaper without any trouble. I was in Germany in 1916. I worked in a hospital tending wounded German soldiers."

"But how, why..."

Wehner continued. "My father had an import-export business with offices in Boston and Hamburg. We happened to be in Hamburg on business in 1916. At that time America was neutral. We were going to be there for several months and I needed something to do, but I wasn't going to work in any armament plant or anything like that. So I went to work for the International Red Cross and they assigned me to a military hospital."

"Oh," Luke said.

"You can see why some people would feel that it wasn't the most patriotic thing to do?"

"Yes, but you did enlist in the American Army and take flight training and all. Why would you do that if you were a German sympathizer?"

"Think Frank. I could be a spy. I could just be waiting for a chance to desert and hand over to the Germans a new Spad for flight testing. Or, I could be waiting to let them know about the big push that's coming up at Chateau Thierry. I wouldn't even have to desert to do that. I could just drop messages when I was over the German lines."

"Surely no one would believe that."

"I've been investigated twice by the Secret Service," Wehner said resignedly. "For all I know, they could be watching me now."

"Watching for what?"

Wehner laughed. "When we were training at San Antonio, they were counting the spoonfuls of sugar that I put into my coffee."

"What for?"

"Ordinarily," Wehner said. "I take my coffee with just a little milk or cream, but some mornings I wake up with a headache and it seems to help if I drink my coffee with some sugar in it, so I put in a spoonful or two. If I have a bad headache I may have sugar in a second or even third cup. On the other hand, if the headache goes away after I drink the first cup with sugar in it, I usually take the second without it. They tried to see a pattern in this. You know, three spoonfuls, three flights the previous day, anything like that."

"But how did you find out about it?"

Wehner laughed again. "I happened to notice one morning this officer that wasn't attached to any of our units making a mark on a piece of paper every time I took a spoonful of sugar. It just so happened that that same day, two airplanes collided when they were landing. The pilots weren't hurt, but the planes were destroyed. The next morning I put seven spoonfuls of sugar in my coffee and, sure enough, they called me in and demanded to know what was going on."

"And they didn't believe you when you explained it to them?"

"I didn't explain anything," Wehner said. "I couldn't. If they knew about the headaches, they would probably take me off of flying status. I told them to go to Hell. By then my flying was so good that Hartney wouldn't let them eliminate me over anything that stupid, but still, it left a question in a lot of people's minds. Some said I could fly so well because I had already learned in Germany. The rumor even went around that I had been an ace in Richthofen's Flying Circus under another name."

"Well," Luke said. "I believe you. I'm glad to room with you. And if it's outcasts, well that's the way it will be."

"Jesus, Frank," Wehner reached out and took his hand again. "You're a spot of sunshine in a gloomy day. A couple of hours ago I was sitting in a corner all alone, thinking about what had happened to McArthur and the others and about what would happen to the squadron when Grant took over, and feeling sorry for myself and then you show up and in ten minutes you have insulted every man in the place and then shut them up by knocking O'Donnel on his ass. All of a sudden, I'm thinking that we may make something out of this war yet."

Luke took his things out of his bags and began to put them away in one of the dressers. Wehner poured himself another drink and lay back and put his feet up on the end of his bed. There was the sound of voices in the hall and of doors being opened and closed.

"Hartney and Grant must be back," Wehner said. "Grant doesn't approve of drinking and late hours, even when we aren't flying the next day."

"Should I let one of them know that I'm here?" Luke asked.

"It'll wait for morning," Wehner told him. "I'll scout for you and let you know when Grant is out of headquarters so that you can report to Hartney. He won't be moving up to group for at least a week, maybe even longer. Something big is cooking above Chateau Thierry. He won't leave until it's over. Be sure to tell him about all your time on the Spad. He may get you checked out in time to get in on it."

"Checked out?" Luke asked.

"Standard procedure," Wehner answered. "You get a tour of the local area with all the landmarks and the other fields pointed out and then Grant gives you your first taste of combat and humiliates you in front of the whole squadron."

"What do you mean?"

"Grant does all of the check outs and, at the end of the flight, he brings you back over the field and the two of you separate and come back around and pass by each other headed in opposite directions and then you each try to get on the others tail. You make the standard climbing turn into the other airplane that they taught you at Issoudun and so does Grant, only he holds his climb just a second or two longer than you can and forces you to turn under him and the next thing you know he's locked on to your tail and there is nothing that you can do to shake him."

"What makes you so sure of that?"

"Because I've seen him do it a dozen times," Wehner said. "He's the best pilot I've ever seen and he flies the best airplane in the squadron and you'll be in old number six."

"He's done this to you?"

"No, just to the new pilots that we've been assigned since we've come from the states. He says he wants to show them just how easy it is to get killed if they're not careful. That makes a certain amount of sense, but if that was all there was to it, he wouldn't have to do it right over the field with all the other pilots and the mechanics watching."

"The best pilot you've ever seen?" Luke questioned. "And you say he's a coward?"

"Yes," Wehner answered. "That's the irony of it. If the man could take a shot of guts every morning when he got up, he could easily have a half dozen victories a month. As it is, in three months, he's got two that he managed to slip up behind without being seen. How can you have any respect for a man like that?"

"Before McArthur went down I thought there was some hope. He was so slick. Just two weeks ago the two of us trailed a formation of eight Fokkers for miles until they were just crossing their lines, headed for ours, and then we dropped down and pulled up under the last two and flamed them both and dove for our own lines before the others could even make a move. Grant won't even attack when we have both the advantage of altitude and numbers."

. Luke finished putting his things away in the dresser and they went down the hall to the latrine. Back in the room they stripped off their clothes and got into bed and Wehner pulled the string by his bed that turned off the light. The rain pounded on the roof harder than ever.

They were silent for a long time; Wehner had almost dropped off to sleep when Luke said abruptly, "You'll see, none of what you told me about the squadron will make any difference to me. I won't let it. I'll either come home an ace or in a box."

Chapter 3

☆ ☆ ☆

On the 26th of July the weather began to clear and the Ameri can Army went over to the offensive for the first time when it counterattacked at Chateau Thierry and attempted to force a crossing of the river Ourcq. Spearheading the American advance was the Rainbow Division commanded by Brigadier General Douglas MacArthur. Defending for the Germans was the elite Prussian Guard commanded by the Kaiser's nephew.

For almost a week, the battle hung in the balance as the two armies locked together in what was to be the turning point in the war. For days, until the Americans could secure both banks, the Ourcq ran red with the blood of both armies.

In the air, the battle was almost as desperate as each side sought to spy out the movements of the enemy and, at the same time, to deny the enemy any knowledge of their operations. For the 27th, the first two days were a disaster. O'Donnel and Elliot fell the first day and Hunt and Sands the second. Wehner and several others returned with machines riddled with bullets and yet, for all the combats, the 27th was unable to confirm a single victory against Udet's red nosed Fokkers. On the third day of the battle, the beaten 27th was ordered to stand down.

In the calm after the storm, Hartney and Grant began to reassemble a squadron out of a remnant of badly shaken veterans and a group of apprehensive new arrivals. Twenty six pilots typically made up a squadron; continued losses of ten a month gave each new pilot a statistical life expectancy of something short of three months. Actually, it was less than that. The first five or six patrols were the critical ones where the losses were the highest. If a new pilot could get through them, learn to hold his place in formation and to take evasive action when attacked, then he might have a chance to go on and score victories himself.

For Luke the days were a torment. Few new aircraft were brought forward from the factories and the work went slowly on the aircraft that had been damaged. There was neither the time nor the aircraft to check out the new pilots. A typical day's flying might consist of a patrol of four aircraft in the morning and four again in the afternoon.

"Damn it, Joe," he said to Wehner one evening. "I'd be better off ferrying aircraft to the front. At least I'd be flying."

"Patience," Wehner consoled him. "Fritz isn't flying any more than we are since Chateau Thierry. He lost two of his forward fields and I suspect he has some wounds of his own to lick. We'll get you up in time for the next big show."

At that, Luke could only shrug his shoulders. But the next day a list of check out rides was posted on the bulletin board and he was scheduled for the second ride, the afternoon of the following day.

The first check out flight fell to a Lieutenant Spalding and Wehner and Luke were both out on the field to watch him take off on Captain Grant's wing. Luke noted that Spalding made a good take off and quickly tucked his aircraft into close formation.

A little more than a half hour later, they reappeared over the field at about four thousand feet and Luke had his first look at the great Captain Grant in action. As Wehner had told him, the two aircraft separated, then came back directly at each other and, as they passed, each pulled up into a climbing turn, trying to get on the tail of the other. Exactly as Wehner had predicted, Spalding's plane stalled and fell off on one wing as Grant passed easily over the top of him. As Spalding rolled the wings level and dropped the nose to regain flying speed, Grant flicked his aircraft over ever so delicately and placed it directly behind the helpless Spalding.

In spite of being forewarned by Wehner of what to expect, Luke could only marvel at the effortless way in which Grant had put himself behind Spalding. Spalding, seeing Grant directly behind him, dove and climbed and turned in an effort to shake him, but it was no use. There was nothing that Spalding could do that Grant had not seen a dozen times before. For ten minutes he sat as tightly on his tail as if the two aircraft had been roped together.

Finally, tiring of his sport, Grant flew up along Spalding and gave the signal to land. The two aircraft spiraled down, crossed behind the buildings and then turned into the wind and landed.

They taxied up to the line and Grant pulled his helmet and goggles off as he shut down the engine. He was all smiles. He had notched another victory witnessed by all of the pilots and ground crew.

"See anything different than what I told you about?" Wehner asked.

"He made it seem so easy," Luke said. "How does he do it?"

"Come along to the mess," Wehner answered. "Lunch will be served in a few minutes. You can listen to him explain all about it."

"No," Luke said. "I want to talk to Spalding a minute."

He walked down to the end of the line where a not too happy looking Spalding was getting out of old number 6. He nodded to acknowledge Luke's presence, but he said nothing.

"What happened up there?" Luke asked.

"What the hell do you mean, what happened?" Spalding snapped. "You were watching. You saw what happened."

"Yes, but he was a good twenty feet above you in the first turn."

"Twenty feet," Spalding snorted. "Twenty feet. It might have been a hundred. There's no way you can climb with him in this piece of junk." He kicked the tail skid for emphasis.

Luke was silent, almost afraid to speak.

"This thing is worse than anything I ever flew at Issoudun."

"How is that?"

"How is that? Let me count the ways." Spalding went on sarcastically. "In the first place, the engine is a hundred RPMs low at take off and toward the end I swear it was dropping out a couple of cylinders. The poor thing wouldn't pull a sick whore off a piss pot."

He paused to catch his breath. "Then there's the controls. It's been crashed and hard and put back together by beginners. You can't make a decent right turn with the rudder pushed clear to the stop, but left is another story. It goes left so quick you can't believe it, but when you go to roll out it takes full right stick and rudder and then it just wallows. You can bet that my Senator will hear about this."

'Good luck with the censor,' Luke thought as Spalding walked away. The crew chief had come up while they were talking, but hearing Spalding's tirade had kept his distance. Luke walked over to where he stood by the wing. "This your airplane corporal?"

"Yes sir. For now sir."

"The Lieutenant had some very uncomplimentary things to say about it."

"Most of them are probably true, sir. This airplane isn't anyone's responsibility. It just get passed around to whoever doesn't have a plane at the time."

"But it's yours now?"

"Yes, for the next few days at least."

"Then I'd think you'd want to do something about the engine at least. Or was Lieutenant Spalding wrong in what he said?"

"No sir, he was right. It's just that there isn't anything that I can do."

"How so?"

"Old number 6 never is sent up on combat patrols. Because of that we can't draw any new parts for it without a written approval from Captain Grant. Even if we could get new plugs, it would start to foul them in a flight or two. And what he said about the rigging is true, but it would take six men a day to just try and straighten it out and then there would be no guarantee that it would be any better than it is now."

"Well, let's have a look at the engine anyway," Luke said. "Bring your tool kit and we'll have the cowling off in a minute and see what there is to be seen."

"Begging your pardon, sir, but lunch is being served at the enlisted men's mess. If I don't go along in a minute, I'll miss mine," the Corporal said apologetically.

"Go along then," Luke said. "Just leave me your tools."

"Oh, I couldn't do that. I couldn't allow anyone to work on the airplane unless it was under my direct supervision. I'm responsible."

"And I have to fly this sorry excuse of an airplane this afternoon," Luke said. "If the engine cuts out on take off, just over the trees at the end of the field, you'll be responsible, but I'll be dead. Now my life is more important to me than my lunch, so I'm going to stay here and have the cowling off. You do as you please, but don't tell me that I can't work on a plane that I'm going to fly."

"But sir, you don't understand, these engines are complicated. Just anyone can't work on them. I'm not even a certified engine mechanic myself."

"Then watch and you may learn something," Luke said as he took off his coat and rolled up his sleeves.

Reluctantly, the corporal opened up his tool box and got out the wrenches they needed and began to help Luke remove the cowling. In a minute it was set aside and the massive Hispano-

Suiza V-8 engine with its sixteen spark plugs and jungle of ignition wires was exposed. "Spark plug wrench," Luke said like a surgeon asking for a scalpel. The corporal obediently passed it to him and soon Luke had the plug out and in his hand. The electrode was oily and the insulator was covered with a burned black deposit.

"Is this your idea of conscientious maintenance?" Luke demanded. "Doesn't it bother you to send a new pilot up with plugs looking like these, or is it more important that you get your lunch on time than we have decent airplanes to fly."

Chagrined, the corporal looked down at his feet. "Sir, I don't say this as an excuse sir, but only as fact. I'm the crew chief, responsible for the whole airplane. But, as you know, I should have an armorer and an engine mechanic assigned to me. Now I don't have either one. Oh, I can pull the plugs and see that they're fouled as good as you, but I can't get new ones and even if I could, I wouldn't know how to correct the cause."

Luke looked around at four wrecked Spads that were stacked behind the main hanger. "I can see that the engine is out of one of those planes," he said. "But how about the others. Surely one of them must have a better set of plugs than these. Any rule against swapping."

"Why, no sir." The corporal looked as surprised as if he has suddenly grasped Copernicus' theory of the motion of the planets. "Let me give you a hand." He got a wrench and began to pull the plugs from the cylinder head opposite Luke.

"Notice how some of these are much worse than others?" Luke asked when he had removed most of the spark plugs from his side of the engine.

"They're none of them too good, sir," the corporal answered. He had set a box up on the engine and was picking up the fouled plugs.

Luke removed the last spark plug in his cylinder bank and pulled over a step ladder and got up on it to have a better look down into the engine compartment. "Hand me a small rag soaked in gasoline and another larger dry one," he said.

The corporal moved without understanding or asking why and brought what Luke asked. Leaning over the engine, Luke wiped the magnetos clean with the gasoline soaked rag and then wiped them dry with the other. "I thought so," he said finally. "Corporal come and have a look."

The corporal climbed up on the ladder with Luke and looked

where he pointed. With the film of oil and dirt wiped away, the crack in the magneto housing was clear to see. The corporal suddenly came to life. "We'll have to work fast to get this all done for this afternoon's flight," he said. "Stay up here on the ladder and I'll hand you up everything you'll need to pull the magneto. Meanwhile, I'll be pulling the good stuff off of one of the spare engines."

A half hour found the new plugs installed and the magneto being maneuvered into place. "Missed you at lunch, Ed. Never knew you to be so keen on your work." A short stocky Sergeant stood at the foot of the ladder.

"Oh, just in time," the corporal said. "Lieutenant Luke, Sergeant Knight, best engine mechanic in the squadron. We'll just get down off the ladder and let him finish this up and do the timing."

The sergeant was looking at the cracked magneto housing on the bench. "How'd you find this?" he asked.

"The corporal thought that we might have a look at the engine before I flew this afternoon," Luke said quickly. "The lieutenant who flew this morning thought the power wasn't quite what it could have been."

The sergeant took off his jacket and rolled up his sleeves and was soon up on the ladder setting up the magnetos. The corporal stood at the foot of the ladder and handed up tools as required. "Might as well do the whole job," the sergeant said. The corporal handed up a can and a pair of pliers and the sergeant drained the water and dirt out of all the traps in the fuel line.

"Thank you sergeant," Luke said as he held out his hand.

"My hands are all greasy, Lieutenant."

"So are mine."

"I'll be damned if they're not," the sergeant said taking Luke's hand. "Did you ever think you'd see it Ed, an officer with grease on his hands?"

"Sir," the corporal said. "You'd better get cleaned up and into your flying suit. Captain Grant won't be late and he won't like it if you are."

"One more thing," Luke said. "Cut me a piece of thin sheet metal about as big as my hand with one straight edge and put four holes for rivets along the straight edge."

Without asking, they set to work. They were curious to see what other surprises this lieutenant who knew engine mechanics had up his sleeve. When it was ready, he had them rivet the metal piece to the trailing edge of the rudder. Then he carefully bent it about thirty degrees to the left. To their questioning glances he said, "It will help to hold the rudder centered so I won't have to stand on the right pedal all through the flight. After a few flights, I'll get it set so that the rudders will be close to neutral at cruise."

"Better hurry lieutenant," the corporal warned again. "We'll have the engine warmed up and ready as soon as you get back."

Luke went off to the barracks at a dog trot and the corporal turned to the sergeant. "Different sort, ain't he?"

"Ain't he though," the sergeant answered.

On the stroke of two o'clock the two engines barked to life and Luke and Grant taxied their Spads out to the far end of the field so that they might take off into the wind. Grant's follies, as his indoctrination flights for new pilots had come to be called, were always well atttended, for it was rare to see such artistry of flight at such close range. Word had spread through the enlisted ranks though, of this different sort of lieutenant and every man of them had found an excuse to be in a place where he would have a clear view of the action.

Forty minutes took them around the circuit of towns and airfields in their area and over the ugly brown scar in the landscape that, before Chateau Thierry, had been no-man's-land. Then, as briefed, they came back over the field, separated and then flew back toward each other so as to pass at a distance of a hundred feet.

As they passed, Grant pulled up gracefully in a Chandelle to his left that gave him the maximum amount of height and the maximum amount of turn. He looked for Luke over his left shoulder and was surprised to find the sky empty. He leveled off, somewhat awkwardly, and scanned the sky all around. Finally, when he looked below the horizon, he saw Luke diving away at a 45 degree angle and rapidly opening up the distance between them.

Up until that moment, Captain Grant had been somewhat distracted by the thought of the pretty, young French Lieutenant's widow that he was to have dinner with that evening. But now, seeing Luke streaking away from him, he became all business. Never before had any new pilot attempted anything but the standard school response taught at Issoudun. He dropped the nose of his

Spad slightly and turned so that he had a better view of Luke. He was not sure what Luke's game was, but with a thousand foot altitude advantage, Grant was clearly in a position to control the fight. On the ground, there was a gasp from the onlookers as Luke's Spad plunged, seemingly out of control, straight for the center of the field. Almost at the last moment, Luke burst straight upward and then continued over as if to begin a loop. Once over on his back though, Luke rolled out in an Immelman turn and lifted the nose of his Spad so that it pointed directly at the somewhat confused Grant.

Luke continued climbing. Grant circled warily above him, wondering how old number 6 could hang so long on the prop. Always right at the edge of a stall, Luke nevertheless managed to keep the nose of his Spad pointed out ahead of Grant. At least four hundred yards separated the two planes; at that distance, a beginner like Luke represented no threat. But the thought flickered through Grant's mind that an old fox like Udet might, even at that distance, know how much to allow for bullet drop and for forward allowance. In a real fight, he might see the muzzles of the other aircraft light up and hear the bullets ripping through the fabric of his craft. He had the advantage of altitude and yet he had allowed himself to be placed in a position where he could be fired upon and could not return the fire

Enough maneuvering for position. Grant pointed the nose of the Spad down and went directly for Luke. Luke dove also, giving up altitude to gain enough airspeed to take him under Grant. Grant's dive steepened almost to vertical as he attempted to follow Luke. A half roll on Grant's part failed to bring Luke into view and he had to pull out of his dive to avoid putting himself right into the trees. As he pulled up he saw Luke turning to his left below him.

He had him then. A quick, half snap roll to the left put him directly behind Luke and slightly above him. Luke dove for the trees and Grant followed. As Grant tried to line Luke up in his sight, Luke's Spad yawed sharply to the right then turned back to the left. So intent was Grant on centering Luke's Spad in his gunsight that he was unaware that they were below the tops of the tallest trees.

A large barn appeared directly ahead of Luke. He started to the right of it and then flicked the Spad up in a vertical bank to the left and passed his wheels within ten feet of the left side of the barn. Grant, his vision somewhat obscured by Luke's plane, judged it safest to pass to the right of the barn and had started in that direction when he saw the pole derrick and ropes that had been set up to hoist hay up into the barn.

The only chance then was to the left and a pilot with less skill than Grant would have been a dead man. He laid the stick over to the left side of the cockpit and came down on the left rudder pedal with all his strength. The Spad stood up on the left wing tip, the barn disappeared behind the lower right wing and he braced himself for the crash that he hoped would break the landing gear off cleanly.

Instead the shock came from the other side. The left wing seemed to dig in and the plane started a cartwheel to the left. Full right rudder and stick held the plane in the air and it slowly righted itself. It took almost half right rudder to hold the plane straight. Grant cautiously eased the plane up to two hundred feet and looked out to the left to see what the trouble might be. It was clear enough. Snagged in the tip of the lower left wing was some forty feet of clothes line with some of the clothes still flapping on it.

Grant looked around for Luke and did not see him until he looked directly to the rear. The propeller of Luke's Spad spun not ten feet behind Grant's tail. Grant gestured with his hand for Luke to drop back and Luke only grinned. Grant imagined that he could look right down the barrels of the twin Vickers machine guns on Luke's Spad. Because they flew so close to the front, even practice missions were flown with the guns armed. A touch of Luke's finger on the triggers would rip his plane to shreds. He gestured Luke back again and again Luke grinned.

Furious, Grant dove and broke hard to his left and kept turning. Even dragging the clothes line, he had enough of a power advantage to outrun a garbage scow like old number 6. But if that was the case he wondered, why wasn't Luke falling behind. They were down in the tree tops again and when Grant looked ahead he saw that they were about to pass directly over the field. There was no way to avoid it. They crossed at about hanger height with Luke again locked in some ten feet behind Grant. All Grant saw as he looked down was hundreds of up turned faces.

It was no use. With the clothes line dragging on the left wing there was nothing Grant could do to shake Luke. He turned away from the field, came around into the wind and landed. Luke moved up from behind and landed on Grant's wing. Grant taxied up to his hanger, cut the engine and went directly to his quarters with out speaking to anyone. An hour or so later the squadron staff car took him into the village and he did not return until morning.

Luke drew a mixed reception. Some of the new replacements crowded around to hear how he had done it, but the old heads, the ones he had insulted the first night, walked away from the line without speaking. Most of them were not overly fond of Grant, but they cared for Luke even less. All things considered, they would have preferred to see him put in his place the way all the other replacements had been.

Wehner got Luke over to the barracks and into their room as quickly as he could. He brought out the bottle and poured out two glasses and said, "Frank, we only saw part of it. What happened? How the hell did you do it? Did this have something to do with your missing lunch? One of the enlisted men said that you did something to the engine on old number 6?"

Luke smiled. "We put new plugs and a new magneto in the engine and that helped a lot. But after seeing what he did to Spalding, I knew that I could never beat him in the air, so I thought that I might change the odds a little by making him fight right in the tree tops."

"But what happened? Where did he get that clothes line and the clothes?"

"We flew right through a farm yard. I almost hit a barn. I don't know how he missed it. That must have been when he snagged the clothes line with his wing. After that, I had him."

"God damn Frank, you are a wonder." Wehner downed his drink and poured himself another. He held out the bottle to Luke. Luke shook his head.

They lay back on their beds and put their feet up. Luke took a few sips of his drink and set it on the floor. Both wanted to talk, but there seemed to be nothing to say. What Luke had done made anything that either one could say irrelevant.

Finally Wehner, after his third drink, spoke again. "God damn Frank, you are a wonder," he said. "If you keep on at this rate, we are in for some high times."

After supper that night, as Luke and Wehner were coming down the steps of the officers' mess a figure stepped out of the twilight and said, "Lieutenant Luke sir, could I have a word with you sir?" It was Corporal Kelly, the crew chief on old number 6.

"Well yes, I guess so," Luke said.

"See you in the barracks, Frank," Wehner said as he went on down the path.

"So what can I do for you corporal? If I knew your name, I'm sorry to say that I've forgotten it."

"It's Kelly, sir," he said moving off to the side of the officer's mess. "I'd like you to meet Corporals Smith and Kline." Two figures stepped out of the shadows. "Corporal Smith is an armorer and Corporal Kline is a certified engine mechanic."

"Well, yes," Luke said. "Glad to meet you." He shook each man's hand.

There was a sort of an awkward silence then until Kelly went on. "Sir," he said. "We'd like to be your new crew."

"On that canvas coffin, old number 6?"

"Oh no sir," Kelly was quick to reassure him. "There are six new Spads coming from the factory tomorrow. They don't even have guns installed. One of them could be yours."

"What makes you so sure of that?"

"We talked to Sergeant Major Muller sir. He said if you were willing to have us, we could pick out one of the new planes."

"Captain Grant might have something to say about that."

"Not tomorrow sir. Major Hartney is officially the squadron commander until midnight tomorrow. He'll sign the order before he goes up to group headquarters."

"You seem awfully sure of this."

"Yes sir. We know certain things. And sir," Kelly went on. "We were the crew for Lieutenant McArthur. He never had any complaints about our work. He was our leading ace before he went down."

"I know," Luke said. "Lieutenant Wehner's told me a good deal about him. If you suited him, I'm sure you'll suit me."

"Then we're agreed sir?"

Luke nodded. "Corporal, what did you have for desert tonight?"

The three men looked at Luke as if he had suddenly lost his senses. "Why, bread pudding," Kline finally managed to say.

"Wait for me out back," Luke gestured toward the officer's mess. "I'll only be a few minutes."

Luke went around to the front of the officer's mess, in the front door and back into the kitchen. "That was wonderful apple pie we had tonight," he said to no one in particular. The cooks all looked around at him.

"I wonder if I could get some more of that pie?" he asked. No one seemed to be able to say a word. Except for the surgeon doing his health inspections, an officer had never been in the kitchen.

Luke looked around and saw a whole pie on one of the pantry shelves. "How about that one?"

The cooks all frowned. They had intended to eat it themselves. Officers had no business in their kitchen.

"What do you say?" Luke continued. "Twenty francs for the whole thing?"

The cooks grinned. Twenty francs would buy a half dozen bottles of cheap wine.

Luke paid and took the pie and went out the back door to where the three corporals were waiting. He put the pie into the astonished Kelly's hands. "I'll tell you something," he said. "It's a lot easier to divide a pie into four pieces than three. I'd sleep better if I knew that Sergeant Major Muller had the fourth piece. As long as I'm to have a new Spad, I'd just as soon have the best of the lot."

"Yes sir," Corporal Kelly said. "I think that we will get on very well together."

The three corporals watched as Luke made his way back to the officer's quarters.

"Different sort, ain't he?" Kline said.

"Ain't he though," Kelly answered.

Chapter 4

☆ ☆ ☆

New Spads arrived and, as Corporal Kelly had promised, one went to Luke. The Vickers guns were installed and sighted. An entire day was devoted to readjusting the tension on all the guy wires and control cables. Sergeant Knight came by the following morning and helped them to coax the last few horsepower out of the engine.

In the end, it was the best Spad that Luke had ever flown. It was quick and light on the controls with no tendency to roll faster one way than the other and it climbed effortlessly. In a dive, it accelerated quickly and was steady as a rock right up to its maximum speed.

Captain Grant seemed to recover his composure and the checkouts of the new pilots continued. Then, one of the new men tried to duplicate what Luke had done and flew old number 6 into a tree and broke his nose and his arm and sent the airplane to the scrap yard. After that, every combat on the checkout flight had to begin with the standard school maneuver of a climbing turn into the attack and Captain Grant stopped his practice of performing directly over the field.

The squadron became operational and once again began to fly combat patrols, but they were restricted to the American side of the lines. Their sole purpose was to prevent the Germans from sending observation planes across the lines and the Germans seemed to have no desire to do that.

Almost every day, Luke got a combat patrol in which they flew down along the front for forty five minutes and then turned around and covered the same area on the way back. There were never any German planes on either side of the line. The guns were fired only in practice.

The new Executive Officer came. His name was Jerry Vasconcelles and his records showed that he had three confirmed victories. He was a short, tough little man with an unlit cigar usually clamped between his teeth. He went about his business in a no nonsense sort of way that demanded a certain amount of respect.

The lack of action was a torture to Luke. Almost every evening in the mess, one of the old boys that had been there the night he arrived would remind him that he was making a slow start for someone who was going to be an ace in his first month at the front. He wished he hadn't been so quick to speak. He had had no idea that a week or more could go by without any combats by any of the squadrons in Hartney's group.

Then, at the morning briefing on the 16th of August, Grant announced that they would send a patrol of eight aircraft over the German lines toward Sossions. There were plans to begin photo reconnaisance flights into the area, but first they wanted to see what kind of response a flight so deep into enemy territory would bring. Grant was to lead the first flight of four and Vasconcelles the second. Miracle of all miracles, Luke was to fly as Vasconcelles' wing man.

The flight was set for mid-afternoon so that they might have the advantage of the sun at their backs on the way in. Luke was down to the line to check on his plane a half dozen times that morning and he was hardly able to contain himself at lunch. "Joe, this is my day," he said a little bit too loudly to Wehner. "I'll get one today, I know it."

"Ha," someone across the table answered. "There's probably some German pilot saying the same thing at this very minute. Someone with a dozen victories already, maybe. You could be number thirteen."

There was a round of a sort of nervous laughter. What the speaker had said was true and some of the pilots assigned to the mission were not particularly anxious to be reminded of it. They would venture almost four miles into enemy territory and fly along parallel to the front line for thirty minutes. If the Germans reacted quickly enough, they might be able to put up double their number and cut them off from the allied lines. Then they would have to fight their way home or run out of fuel and make forced landings in enemy territory.

Luke had no such reservations. "You'll see," he said. "If we get a fight, I'll come home with a victory or not at all."

The entire squadron came out to watch the take off, enlisted men as well as officers. Grant was off first with his flight of four and thirty seconds later Vasconcelles signaled for full power for his flight. As Luke pushed the power up, the engine stumbled and almost died. He pulled it back to idle and checked the gauges. Oil pressure was up and the temperature needle was steady in the center of the gauge. Air pressure was low, almost down to nothing. Kelly and Klein had run up on either side of the plane when they had heard it miss and they leaned into the cockpit. "Tank pressure's low," Luke shouted as he pointed at the gauge.

"Hand pump!"

Luke worked the hand pump and the needle on the gauge began to rise slowly.

"Now push the power up."

He advanced the power to about half and Kelly and Klein held on to the edge of the cockpit to keep the plane from moving forward. The engine driven pump began to boost the air pressure in the main fuel tank. Vasconcelles and the other two aircraft were already lifting off the ground at the far end of the field.

"Lot of fuel in the tank and not much room for air," Klein shouted. "You should be all right as soon as you burn off a little fuel."

Luke looked toward Kelly. "What do you think?"

"If you can hold this much pressure at full throttle, go ahead. Just keep your eye on it for the first hundred yards. If the pressure starts to drop, chop the throttle, cut the switches and ground loop it if you have to."

Luke nodded and pulled his goggles down over his eyes. Vasconcelles and the other two planes in the last flight were disappearing over the trees at the end of the field. Kelly and Klein stood clear and Luke pushed the throttle forward to the stop. The engine turned a full 2,000 RPMs and held and soon he was airborne and climbing after the flights ahead of him.

There was only a light haze and Luke could see not only Vasconcelles, but Grant and his flight of four ahead of them. He reduced the RPMs to 1,800 and checked on the air pressure. It was holding steady, but still lower than normal. The water temperature had risen some and he opened the radiator shutters a notch. He was closing slowly on Vasconcelles. If he caught them by the time they reached the lines, they could fly the mission as planned.

They crossed the old lines, now an empty and abandoned waste land, and kept on climbing for their briefed altitude of 8,000 feet. Puffy clouds appeared at their level as they neared the new lines and Luke was having trouble keeping Grant in sight, although Vasconcelles and the other two behind Grant were still clearly visible, now less than a quarter mile in front of him.

The clouds grew thicker and Grant and Vasconcelles began to alter their courses almost continuously to keep their flights in the clear. Luke pushed the power up to full again to close with Vasconcelles, but when he did, the main tank air pressure began to slowly drop. He reduced power again and began to consider turning back. He looked down through the broken clouds beneath him to try and fix his position and saw nothing familiar. When he looked back at the air pressure, it was slowly increasing.

By then they had crossed the German lines and he abandoned the idea of returning. If he returned, the engine would run flawlessly all the way home and he would be ridiculed in the mess for turning back from his first trip over the lines in a perfectly good ship. He concentrated on keeping Vasconcelles in sight and in cutting off as much distance as he could by taking the inside of the turns. Periodically, he tried to push the power up to full and every time he did, the air pressure dropped. Still he was closing the distance. Vasconcelles was little more than a hundred yards ahead of him and just beginning his turn to the heading that would parallel the front. The first time one of the flight looked around to clear their tails, they would see him.

Then, as he looked around to clear his own tail, he saw a German two seater pass not more than three hundred feet above him on an easterly heading. It was painted solid silver and the black crosses stood out distinctly on the wings. As it went away from him he saw that it had a unique biplane tail. It was all alone and it gave no sign that it had seen him or any of the other ships in the formation. If Vasconcelles would only look back, he could lead him to the two seater. It would be an easy victory for someone.

He rocked his wings in the hope that someone would see him, hesitated for only a second, and then turned to follow the two seater. In less than a minute, Vasconcelles and Grant were out of sight behind the clouds and he was alone with the two seater slightly above him and out ahead of him some four hundred yards. With full power he could have caught him quickly, but he had to nurse the engine along, pulling full power for ten or twenty seconds and then reducing it to let the air pressure build back up. As much as possible, he kept some cloud between himself and the two seater. If they saw him before he was close enough to fire, they might dive into one of the clouds and escape.

Minutes passed with the two seater leading Luke directly away from the lines. The Germans seemed to be unconcerned about the possibility of enemy aircraft so deep in their own territory. Luke slowly crept up behind them. Then, to his amazement, when he pushed the power up the air pressure not only held, but actually climbed toward the center of the gauge. It was his chance.

The two seater was passing just to the left of a small puffy cloud and Luke, with the engine running flat out, dropped the nose for even more speed and went straight into the cloud. It was a forbidden maneuver. A pilot could easily lose his balance and have the plane fall out of control, but the best pilots did it, for short periods of time. The trick was to sit perfectly still and hold the rudder and the ailerons steady and to use the elevator to keep the altimeter from increasing or decreasing.

He counted the seconds, ten, twenty, thirty; the cloud was larger than he had guessed. The altimeter dropped a hundred feet and he increased the pressure on the stick with his little finger. The altimeter began to settle and he held the pressure he had. The instrument lagged several seconds behind his actual altitude. To chase it would set up a roller coaster series of climbs and dives that could throw the airplane out of control.

Forty seconds, fifty seconds, he could no longer be sure that the wings were level. If one wing were down, the plane would be turning. To look down at the compass on the floor could throw off any sense of balance he had left and that instrument typically lagged behind the actual reading even more than the altimeter. He managed to sneak a glance at the air pressure gauge. It was steady in the center of the dial.

Then suddenly he was out into an almost blinding sunshine. He looked around quickly for the two seater. It was nowhere to be seen. They had turned or outwitted him by flying into a cloud themselves. And then he looked up. The two seater was directly above him, not fifty feet away. He could see the rear gun hanging from the mount and the observers gloved hand over the side of the cockpit. The observer was facing forward. They had no idea that there was another airplane within miles of them.

Luke's heart began to pound. He took a deep breath as Wehner had taught him and forced himself to concentrate. He pulled the power back slightly and, as he began to drop behind the two seater, he gradually raised the nose of his Spad. When his gunsight steadied just ahead of the propeller of the two seater, he pulled both triggers and let the sight drift back along the bottom of it as the twin Vickers hammered away. Pieces of fabric and wood were ripped away and blown back in the slip stream, but the two seater flew steadily onward. He fired again and this time a large piece of silver fabric separated from the underside of the two seater. It took no evasive action; the rear gun was not moved from the stowed position.

Cautiously, Luke eased his Spad up and forward so that he could see into the cockpits of the two seater. Both the pilot and the observer were slumped over. They were dead, but the engine continued to run and the aircraft flew on in a straight line. Pulling up slightly, Luke fired into the engine at almost point blank range. There were two puffs of black smoke and then the propeller stopped. The two seater nosed over and began a long spiraling dive toward the ground. It did not burn.

Luke followed it part of the way down and saw it crash in a triangular shaped wood about five miles from a good sized town. He had no idea where he was, but he fixed the town and the roads and the railroads that ran out of it in his mind. So intent was he on remembering the details of the area that it was a full minute before it registered in his mind that he had gained his first victory and killed his first Germans. And it had been easy. They had not been keeping their eyes open. They had never known what had hit them.

Suddenly, he realized that for several minutes he had not been keeping his eyes open. He looked quickly back over his shoulder and above and below, sure that some Fokkers must be closing on him. Except for his Spad the sky was empty. The Hispano-Suisa in front of him ran effortlessly, the air pressure was up, the oil pressure was steady and the water temperature only slightly cooler than normal. He took another deep breath and set himself to thinking about his next course of action.

He was in some trouble. The gauge on the main fuel tank showed that it was a little more than half full and he was deep in enemy territory. He had only a rough idea of where he was and the clouds kept him from seeing any prominent landmarks. He did not want to descend below the clouds. If attacked, he wanted to be able to duck into one. He had enough ammunition left for another fight, but not the fuel. He guessed that it was going to take all he had to get home. If the wind out of the west was particularly strong, he might be lucky just to make it back across the lines.

He came around to a heading of southwest and climbed back up to 8,000 feet. At that level he had a chance of seeing the rest of the flight and joining them for the return over the lines. Also, if he saw any Fokkers, he could drop the nose and trade some of his altitude for airspeed and run away from them.

He throttled back to his most efficient power setting of 1,600 RPMs and watched the ground through the breaks in the clouds to see if he could locate any landmark that would give him his position. As he made his way along a great canyon of clouds that stretched a good 5,000 feet above, and below him, he felt a strange sense of loneliness that he had never felt before in any of his flights.

His Spad seemed so small and insignificant in the great expanse of sky and clouds that spread out around him. He had never flown so high, either in training or in France. His ferry flights had all been at a thousand or two thousand feet. Now, in his glimpses of the ground through the clouds, everything seemed to be in miniature.

He was a mile and a half high. Farmers, working out in their fields, might look up and see his Spad as a dark speck against the clouds, but it was unlikely that they could hear the sound of his engine. Lost and alone, he somehow had the sense that he had ceased to exist along with the men in the two seater. He would not begin to exist again until he was safely back on the ground at Saints.

Ahead of him and off to his left, through a break in the clouds, he could see a large city with the tall spires of a cathedral sticking up. He searched over his map. It could only be Reims. He was farther east than he had imagined. He turned another thirty degrees to the west and went on.

The minutes went by and he crossed what had to be the river Vesle. The river ran from Reims to Soissons, but he could not see Soissons because of the clouds. Four aircraft, too far away to appear as much more than dots, crossed in front of and below him.

The clouds began to thin out and he saw what appeared to be a large tent city laid out in a square. He was sure he was getting close to the lines. He pushed the power up to 1,800 RPMs and dropped the nose slightly to let the airspeed build. If he was to meet Fokkers, it would most likely be close to the lines.

The clouds broke up and he could see that he was coming up on the lines. Far to the west, German anti aircraft gunners were firing at a flight of several aircraft. He wondered if it could be Grant and Vasconcelles.

Just at that moment the engine cut out completely. He glanced quickly at the air pressure gauge and saw that it was at zero. He frantically worked the hand pump and saw the pressure slowly begin to rise. Finally, after what seemed like several minutes, the engine caught again, but he had lost two thousand feet of altitude. He was directly over the German lines, but the gunners either had not seen him or did not want to waste ammunition on a single plane.

He crossed the American lines and the engine died again. The engine driven pump was no longer supplying any pressure. He worked the hand pump again, and again the pressure in the tank came up and the engine caught and then died. The main tank was almost empty. He gave it up and switched over to the gravity fed emergency tank in the upper wing. It held only a gallon of fuel, but that would be enough to allow him to pick a good field and to make his approach under power. He still did not know where he was.

And then, directly head of him was an airfield with several large hangers. At least two dozen Spads were parked along the flight line. It was the French field, the home of the famous Storks. He crossed over the field at a thousand feet and saw two Spads with French markings turn under him and begin their final approach. He pulled his throttle back to idle and started a long sweeping turn that brought him in directly behind them.

In little more than a minute he was down and taxiing across the grass behind the other Spads. Two crewmen ran out on to the field and signaled him in to a parking space. The one grabbed on to the tail to stop him when he was in the proper place and the other, out in front of him, gave him the signal to switch off the engine.

The propeller jerked to a stop and the two French mechanics came up to help him out of the cockpit. They saw that the guns had been fired and the one pointed to them and asked something in French. He shook his head, "No parle Frances."

The other made a sign with his hand of an aircraft spinning down and crashing. He nodded and held up one finger. The two Frenchmen smiled broadly. "Bien, tres bien," the one said.

Back at Saints, Grant and Vasconcelles and the rest were safely down and they were astonished to hear that Luke had taken off and tried to catch them, for none of them had seen him. Corporal Kelly explained what had happened with the engine and what Luke had intended to do. Grant was furious with Luke for his having decided to try and catch the flight when his take off was delayed for so long. Vasconcelles was equally furious with Kelly and Klein for encouraging him to go so far across the lines with an engine that was obviously giving trouble. Hard words passed between all concerned. Having lost ten pilots in July, the 27th had gone more than two weeks in August without a single fatality. A loss now, on a mission when no enemy aircraft had been sighted, would be a bad omen.

A phone call to a forward observation post revealed that they had seen four Spads, closely followed by three others with a fourth trailing by a quarter of a mile, cross the lines and disappear into enemy territory. No observation post had reported seeing a single ship return. Considering the amount of fuel that they had all had, Luke was for certain down somewhere.

Minutes passed. Luke's crew, disconsolate, stood off by themselves in a little group. Wehner sat alone by himself. The other officers wandered along the flight line, remembering what Luke had said about coming back with a victory or not at all. Most were angry at him for being the one to start a new string of losses.

Then the orderly came running out of headquarters calling out for Captain Grant. Everyone gathered around him. "Major Hartney called, from Group Headquarters," he blurted out. "They heard from Luke. He's down safe."

"Where? How?" Grant demanded.

"He tried to call here, but he couldn't get through direct so he called Group and spoke to Major Hartney. He's down at the Storks. The air pump on the engine is out and the French mechanics won't have it fixed before dark. Major Hartney told him to stay the night and come back in the morning."

"He didn't say where Luke had been or what had happened?" Vasconcelles wanted to know.

"No sir," the orderly replied. "I've told you all that Major Hartney told me."

"We'll hear some Cock and Bull story when he gets back tomorrow," Grant said sourly. "At least, I won't have to sit down tonight and write his mother and tell her what a brave boy her son was."

Chapter 5

L uke returned after breakfast. His mechanics were quick to apologize for having sent him off across the lines with a malfunctioning engine. It was the first problem that Luke had had with the airplane and they were uncertain as to how he might feel about it.

He explained that the diaphragm in the pump had been installed incorrectly when it was manufactured and that a tear had developed and gradually spread until the pump could no longer function. He did not seem especially upset over having had to land at the Storks and to spend the night with them.

Smith, the armorer, was the first to notice that the guns had been fired. Luke told them what had happened, but pledged them to secrecy until he could make his official report. Smith quickly removed the ammunition belts from the guns and set about cleaning them. Klein and Kelly pulled the cowling so that they could inspect the repair work that the French mechanics had done.

When he had come in to land, Luke had noticed that most of the Spads were gone. At the operations office he found out that Captains Grant and Vasconcelles, along with most of the rest of the squadron had flown up to inspect the field at Rembercourt. Rembercourt had never been held by the Germans, but they had shelled it during their offensive and forced the French to abandon it. Now, since the American offensive at Chateau Thierry, it was beyond the range of the biggest German guns. If the engineers could put it into operating condition without too much work, it would become the new home of the 27th.

Luke got the forms and sat down at one of the briefing tables in operations and filled out a combat report for the day before. At the Storks, with the help of one of the French pilots who spoke English and knew the area, he had worked his way backward on the map and had identified the area where the two seater had gone down. The triangular shaped piece of wood lay to the north of the road that ran between Joul and Vailly. Vailly had been the town that he had seen. All the roads and railroads matched.

In an hour or so, Captain Grant and some of the other pilots returned. A half dozen others had gone on to fly a combat patrol and Vasconcelles and Wehner and two other pilots had pushed their planes into one of the hangers that was not wrecked and were waiting at Rembercourt on the chance that they might see a German observation plane go over and be able to take off and surprise it since the field looked to be abandoned.

The morning passed slowly. The flight of six returned and reported that they had not seen another aircraft anywhere. It was not quite time for lunch and the pilots sat out on the benches in front of operations and took some sun.

The door of operations slammed and Captain Grant came down the steps. "Luke, did you submit this report?"

"Yes sir."

The other pilots all turned to look at Grant. Luke had said nothing to them about his victory over the two seater the day before. He had wanted Grant to see the report first.

"Do you expect me to believe this fairy tale?"

"It's not a fairy tale, sir."

"Then what the hell is it?" Grant demanded. "You lose the formation. You get lost yourself and run out of fuel and have to land at the Storks. And then you make up this story. My God, a kid in kindergarten could tell a more believable lie."

The rest of the pilots listened intently. They knew how angry Grant had been when Luke had gone missing the day before. But they could only guess at what was in the report that Grant held in his hand.

"Sir," Luke stood up and faced Grant. "You have no reason nor right to question my report."

"No reason, no reason," Grant grew red in the face. He turned to the second page of the report and read from it. "The Hannoveraner fell into a triangular shaped wood north of the road between Joul and Vailly. How the hell could you know that? Joul and Vailly and the road between aren't even on your map."

"Yes sir. I worked it out on the Ordnance map at the Storks, navigating backward from Reims. I saw Vailly clearly. All the roads and railroads matched with what I remembered. It couldn't have been any other town."

"Navigated backward from Reims? You want us to believe that you were as far as Reims? What makes you think that you were at Reims?"

"I passed just to the west of it. I saw the cathedral clearly."

"Saw the cathedral? Jesus Christ Lieutenant! Every town in Europe has a cathedral. Maybe you were over Strasbourg or Frankfurt? You can reach them from here you know. With a two hundred mile per hour tail wind both coming and going."

From the front door of the officer's mess the cooks looked out to where the officers stood in a group in front of operations. It was time for lunch, but no one was moving.

"Sir," Luke said. "I worked this out very carefully at the Storks. I passed ten miles or so to the west of Reims."

Grant ignored that remark. "And this Hannoveraner that you say you shot down. How did you know what it was?"

"I didn't at the time, sir," Luke said. "But I described it to the Storks and they showed me a picture."

"Enough of this god damned Storks business. You know you can't claim a victory unless it's confirmed by someone on the ground."

"Yes sir, I know. I didn't expect to get credit for it now. But it is a part of my combat report. And after the war is over or after we make an advance, if the wreck of a silver Hannoveraner is found in that wood, then I might get credit."

"Bull Shit," Grant fumed. "This report is nothing but Bull Shit from start to finish. If you can't tell the truth, don't even bother to turn in a report." He threw the papers on the ground and turned and went up the step and into the operations office.

The was a sort of an embarrassed, strained silence and then someone asked, "Was that an equilateral or an isosceles triangle, Lieutenant? There are a lot of woods along that road you know."

There was general laughter at that and some remarks made aside. The pilots got up and started over toward the mess.

"I killed two Germans yesterday while the rest of you were just out joyriding and burning up gasoline," Luke insisted.

They turned their backs and walked away from him. The report lay in the dirt in front of the steps. Luke left it there and went back to his room in the barracks.

It was late in the afternoon before Luke heard the sound of the four Spads returning from Rembercourt. He did not go out to watch them land or to hear if they had flown a combat patrol. After what Grant had said and the way the other pilots had reacted, he had no desire to leave his room. When he had had time to think about it, he realized that he had taken a great risk to gain his first victory and that it had taken a great deal of skill to hold the Spad steady in the cloud for almost a minute. Grant and the other pilots had cheapened it and spoiled it for him by not believing that he could have done it.

It was almost an hour before Wehner came down the hall and into the room. Luke was sitting on his bed with his back against the wall. He had a pen and a writing tablet in his hand.

"Writing home Frank?" Wehner said. "Don't finish it up just yet. I've got some news that you may want to put into it."

"It's not a letter home."

"Oh, to a little girl in San Diego?"

Luke shook his head and threw the tablet over to Wehner. Wehner looked it over carefully. "Request transfer from Flying Service to Infantry," he read aloud. "Bad move, Frank. Winter's coming on. They tell me it's hell in the trenches in winter. Here, at least, it's a hot meal and clean sheets every day you make it back."

"Don't kid about it, Joe," Luke said. "You must have heard about what happened between me and Captain Grant. There isn't any way that I can stay on here."

"I think there is," Wehner said and he proceeded to tear up the request that Luke had written. "I saw your combat report. Good piece of work."

"You believe it?"

"Sure."

"You must be the only one." Luke said bitterly.

"No, not quite." Wehner said smiling. "There's at least one other believer and his opinion is worth more than everybody else's put together."

Luke looked at Wehner questioningly.

"You did tell Hartney that you shot down a two seater when you called him from the Storks yesterday, didn't you?" Wehner asked.

"Well, yes."

"And he didn't say anything about not believing you?"

"No."

"So there you are," Wehner said. "He called and asked that a copy of your combat report be sent up to group as soon as possible. The orderly is typing up a copy this very minute. I was there when the call came in. They had to go out and pick your report up out of the dirt."

"A lot of good that will do me in this squadron," Luke said. "You didn't hear what Grant had to say. You didn't see the way the rest of the pilots turned their backs and walked away from me. No one even wanted to hear my story."

"The hell with them," Wehner answered. "They don't count any more. Everything is different now."

"Like, how?"

"Just listen," Wehner said. "We hung around Rembercourt all morning and at least half of the afternoon. Finally, Vasconcelles decided that we weren't going to see any action there so he decided to fly a combat patrol and then come on home to Saints."

"And you got a fight?"

"We did, but let me tell it like it happened," Wehner said. "Vasconcelles took us up to twelve thousand feet, that's higher than I'd ever been before. The wind was strong up there. Vasconcelles knew that it would be, so we worked west along the lines in order to have the wind at our backs coming home. For the first forty five minutes we didn't see a thing and then, just as we were turning back to the east, we saw two, two seaters at about nine thousand feet and five Fokkers about a thousand feet above them. They sailed across the lines on an almost due south heading. It looked almost too good to be true."

"Now if it had been Grant," Wehner went on. "He would have maneuvered for position or tried to get where he could come directly out of the sun or maybe he would have tried to somehow slip up behind one of the two seaters without being seen. Not Vasconcelles. He took one good look above us to make sure it wasn't a trap and then, down we went. I couldn't believe it. We were actually attacking almost twice our number."

"The minute we started down, the two seaters turned and dove for their lines, but the Fokkers went on as if they hadn't seen us. I was a little on the outside of the turn when we went for them, so I was a little behind the rest in the attack. We were at full throttle, diving at about a forty-five degree angle. We must have been doing two hundred miles an hour and I'm pounding on the edge of the cockpit, screaming, 'faster, faster."

"At the last possible second, they turned right into us and we went through them with all of our guns blazing and all of theirs blazing back. Vasconcelles pulled right up into a big Immelman turn and we all went with him and there they were, coming head on again with all the guns firing. How we avoided a collision, I don't know. I thought I got some shots into one, but he never slowed down."

"For a few seconds it was just a mass of airplanes milling around and then we were all sorted out in a big Luffbury circle. I had a Fokker behind me and another in front. Where the odd Fokker was, I don't know. Before we had gone around twice, I had caught up with the one ahead of me and was able to pull enough lead on him to fire. He immediately snapped over on his back and I hit him again and he caught on fire. He went down in a long spiral with a trail of black smoke behind him."

"As soon as the one went down, the other Fokkers broke for home. We chased them as far as the lines and I think that I got some rounds into another one, but they all made it back into their own territory. Vasconcelles took us back then to where my Fokker had fallen. It was in the middle of a wheat field and it burned a big black circle in the middle of the yellow grain. We might drive out to see it, but I don't think that there would be much left after the fire."

"It will be confirmed though?" Luke said.

Wehner nodded and reached into the cabinet for his bottle of Scotch and two glasses. He poured out two drinks. "Here's to number three."

They tossed their drinks back and Wehner reached out with the bottle to fill Luke's glass again. Luke shook his head.

"Oh, no," Wehner said. "No excuses tonight. We've much to celebrate and no place to go except over to the mess for our supper."

Luke, somewhat reluctantly, held out his glass and Wehner poured two more drinks. "Now, this is to your first victory, unconfirmed though it may be, and to the skill and cunning that it took for you to get it."

They drank again and again Wehner reached out with his bottle for Luke's glass. "No more," Luke protested.

"Last round," Wehner said. "But this is the most important toast of all."

Luke held out his glass and Wehner filled it almost to overflowing. He filled his own as full. "Now, stand at attention and pay attention to the orders of the day," Wehner said, mimicking Captain Grant. "Here's to the new commander of B flight and," Wehner paused for effect. "And his new wing man. Here's to us."

"I can't believe it," Luke said in amazement. "Grant would never do anything like that."

"No, he wouldn't, so drink up and I'll tell you a story." Wehner tipped up his glass and Luke followed suite.

"Grant may be the Squadron Commander, but Vasconcelles is going to have more than a little bit to say about what happens on the flight line and in the air. It seems that he and Hartney go a long way back."

"Where did you hear that?" Luke asked.

"Oh, I had a very interesting talk with one of the engineers at Rembercourt this afternoon while Vasconcelles was taking a nap. It seems that Vasconcelles and Hartney spent some time flying together in the Canadian Air Service before Hartney was shot down and had his legs broken. The two of them made a specialty of going out early in the morning, sometimes before it was light, and flying deep into enemy territory to try and catch the Germans by surprise by attacking from the east, right out of the rising sun. If what the lieutenant told me is true, they each probably have a half dozen or more victories that will never be confirmed.

Luke hung his head down. "To think that I was ready to ask for a transfer to the infantry. And now....."

"And now," Wehner finished for him. "You've got to stay out of trouble and save your fighting for the Germans. I'm your flight commander now. You have any complaint, you come to me first."

Luke gave him a puzzled look.

"No Frank, I mean it this time." Wehner said seriously. "Grant doesn't know yet about my being a flight leader and about your being assigned to me. He won't like it, but if you stay out of trouble and we start knocking down some Fokkers, there won't be anything he can do about it. All of a sudden, I like our chances, but we've got to stick together."

"Together," Luke said, already beginning to feel the effect of the whisky.

"Together," Wehner echoed him. "We'll rise or fall together."

Chapter 6

The squadron moved to Rembercourt and settled in and began flying regular patrols along the front. German activity was light. Most patrols returned without ever having seen an enemy aircraft. In contrast to July, when eight had been killed and two more wounded, August ended without the 27th having lost a single pilot.

With the beginning of September, the weather turned cold and rainy and the number of missions over the enemy lines increased. Something was building in the St. Mihiel sector. On the allied side, troops were massing just behind the lines and the roads were often clogged with artillery columns bogged down in the mud.

On the German side of the lines, there appeared to be less activity, but every observation or photography flight inevitably brought up a swarm of Fokkers. It became necessary to send as many as a dozen escorts for a single observation plane. Clearly, Fritz did not want the Americans to know what he was up to.

The combats were usually short and sharp, the Germans content to withdraw when they had turned the observation planes back. A day seldom passed when Luke did not fire his guns and yet another victory eluded him. Several times he put a stream of bullets into a Fokker, only to have to turn away to avoid becoming a target himself. Two, he felt, must have gone down as the hits were in the engine and cockpit, but he did not see them crash himself and they were too far across the lines for an American observer to have seen them.

Wehner got another victory when they intercepted a flight of eight Fokkers escorting a two seater on a photographic mission over the American lines. Grant was leading the flight of a dozen

Spads of the 27th. He should have gone directly for the Fokkers and the two seater, for he had the advantage of altitude and numbers and his orders were to prevent any observation of the American movements, at all costs. But Grant held on to his altitude, trying it seemed to get up sun.

Wehner, leading the last group of four, saw opportunity slipping away and, on his own initiative, went for the two seater and Luke followed him. The two seater dove away toward the German lines and Wehner switched his attention to the Fokkers who hesitated to commit to his attack because of Grant sitting at an altitude advantage with eight more Spads. One of the Fokker pilots panicked and broke formation and turned for his own lines. Wehner, with the speed he had picked up in his diving attack, quickly closed on the lone Fokker and shot him down with a single long burst.

Grant, seeing the German formation beginning to break up, finally brought his eight Spads down into the attack, but he was too late. The two seater had slipped away and the remaining seven Fokkers turned to face Grant head on. Grant, afraid to trade shots with the Fokkers in a head on pass, pulled his Spads back up above the Fokkers and turned away from the front line. The Fokkers then split into two groups and headed for home. Wehner started for the nearest group and then had to turn back when he realized that, without Grant's eight Spads in support, his attacking either group of Fokkers would leave him and Luke wide open to the other and perhaps trapped on the German side of the lines.

Back on the ground, Wehner was furious. "Jesus Christ, Frank," he screamed in disgust. "We could have had them all. If only Grant had gone through them and got between them and the lines. Then we would have had them boxed in on two sides and outnumbered twelve to seven and everybody but me with full ammunition belts. We won't see another set up like that for the rest of the war."

Grant came walking down the line to where Wehner and Luke were standing by their planes. "Nice shooting, Lieutenant," he said to Wehner. "I guess we sent them home with their tails between their legs."

"Yes sir, we did," Wehner answered. "I only wish that we might have gotten a few more. We had them outnumbered almost two to one."

"We did," Grant answered thoughtfully. "But it's best not to be too greedy, especially when so many of our men are new. Our job was to turn them back and we did that. And do you know, we've gone five weeks now without losing a man or an airplane. I wouldn't want to needlessly risk breaking that string."

"Yes sir, I see." Wehner said.

"Coming along to debriefing?" Grant asked.

"In a minute sir," Wehner answered. "I want to make sure that my guns are rearmed immediately and that the fuel tank is filled. Business seem to be picking up. With your permission, sir, I'd like to have my airplane and three others warmed up every thirty minutes for the rest of the day."

"Seems reasonable enough," Grant said. "See you in operations in a few minutes. You'll want to get your combat report in right away. I'm sure confirmation has already come in."

"Stupid shit," Wehner said, under his breath, when Grant had walked far enough away to be out of hearing. "Doesn't want to be too greedy. Doesn't want to risk breaking his perfect Sunday School attendance record. He'll make cowards of the whole squadron if he can. And then those seven, that we let get away today, will come back tomorrow, or some other day, and shoot the whole bunch of cowards down. I could puke when I think of the chance that Grant threw away this morning because he didn't want to risk his new men. Hell, the Germans have got new men too, probably with a lot less training than you and I have had. Compared to Texas and California, the flying weather in Germany is terrible. If Grant had just pressed his attack, they might have scattered like a bunch of chickens and given everyone a chance for a victory."

The mechanics came up and Wehner gave his orders and he and Luke went off to the briefing. It began to rain heavily soon after lunch and it continued for the rest of the day. The planes were all pushed into the hangers and Wehner sat in his chair in a corner of the mess and sulked. At bedtime he was still complaining about the perfect chance they had missed that morning.

The rainy days continued one right after the other. Whenever the sky would clear, at least partially, both sides sent up observation planes and pursuits. Something big was coming. Every day the road beside the field was filled with infantry moving to the front. Observation balloons were up all along the lines on both sides. Coming back across the lines one afternoon, Luke pointed down at one of the German sausages and Wehner shook his head in answer.

"You know the rule, Frank," Wehner said when they were back on the ground at Rembercourt. "Absolutely no balloons. It's too dangerous. They're ringed with anti aircraft and machine guns."

"I know," was Luke's answer. "But they're so big. They would be impossible to miss. Can you imagine what one would look like, burning."

"Try to imagine what it would be like in the trenches with all this rain," was Wehner's answer. "I can guarantee you that that is exactly where Grant would send you if you made so much as a single pass at one."

Luke shrugged. He knew what Wehner said was true. Still, from that day on, he made a ritual of pointing out every German balloon that he saw and Wehner made a ritual of shaking his head in disapproval.

Early on the morning of September 12th, Wehner and Luke were awakened by a dull rumbling. At first they thought it was thunder in the distance, for outside their window the rain was falling heavily. Wehner lit a match to look at his watch and saw that it was two minutes past three o'clock. Outside, it was pitch dark.

The rumbling continued and it became obvious that it was not thunder, but heavy artillery firing in massed volleys. The Americans were making the opening move in the battle for St. Mihiel. It was no use trying to sleep. Luke and Wehner sat up in bed and speculated on what the day might bring.

There would be no flying, for certain, as long as the rain continued to fall. But if the rain let up, both sides would fill the sky with planes in an effort to see how the battle went and where the reserves were being brought up for a possible counter attack. An hour under such conditions might bring more opportunities than a month spent flying routine patrols.

At four thirty, when it was still dark, an orderly came down the hall and knocked at every door. All the pilots were wanted in operations as soon as possible. Luke and Wehner quickly dressed and took their raincoats and joined the stream of men headed across the muddy compound.

In operations, the pilots found that the cooks had brought over coffee in field containers and also some doughnuts. It was obvious they had been up since the guns had started. Luke and Wehner each got themselves a doughnut and some coffee and found seats against the wall. Luke noticed that Wehner took two spoonfuls of sugar in his coffee.

"Something cooking," Wehner noted. "Hartney isn't down here paying a social call, not at this hour."

Luke looked up to the front of the room where Hartney and Grant and Vasconcelles were talking with their heads together. The last of the pilots came in, got coffee and doughnuts and found themselves seats.

Hartney got up in front of the area map with a pointer and the room fell silent. "As you must have guessed," he said. "Pershing has started his offensive against St. Mihiel, all along the line. The infantry is scheduled to jump off in less than half an hour. As long as this rain keeps up, there is nothing that we can do to help them. But," here Hartney paused. "The rain has already stopped in Paris and it is generally clearing from the west. It should be light enough to fly in a half hour or forty-five minutes, though there will be scattered patches of ground fog."

Hartney paced around with the pointer behind his back. "Here," he put the pointer to the map. "Here, just outside Marieulles, a balloon was put up last evening, just before dark. The Germans have never had one in that vicinity before. Unfortunately, if it is there this morning, and I have every reason to believe that it will be, it will command a perfect view of the main line of our attack."

Hartney paused and put the pointer on the table in front of him. "Now," he continued. "Last night, a request went up from General MacArthur to General Pershing to have that balloon brought down at first light. This morning, the order came down from Pershing, through Colonel Mitchell, to me, to destroy that balloon as soon as it was light enough to do so."

The room was absolutely silent. Doughnuts and coffee cups were suspended in mid air. They waited to hear the who and how of it. Grant looked unusually pale. It would probably fall to him to lead the first attack.

"I want volunteers," Hartney said abruptly.

No one moved. Grant swallowed nervously. If no one volunteered, he must.

"What do say, Frank," Wehner asked. "Do you want it?"

All eyes turned on Luke. His face was expressionless, but he gave the slightest sign of a nod.

"We'll do it then," Wehner said. "As soon as the rain stops and we get a break in the fog."

"Just the two of you?" Hartney asked.

"More would be too hard to keep track of with the visibility likely to be bad," Wehner said. "But I'll want four for top cover if the ceiling is high enough for them to have Fokkers up."

"I'll lead those," Vasconcelles said quickly.

A spirit of excitement ran through the room. A half dozen hands went up as volunteers to fly with Vasconcelles and he picked three. He got the numbers of the six aircraft that were to make up the mission and jotted them down on a slip of paper. "I want these six, plus a spare, armed as soon as possible," he said to the operations clerk. "Full tracer in the right guns and every other round, tracer and ball in the left. As soon as the guns are armed, I want the engines warmed up."

The operations clerk went for the flight line on the double.

Vasconcelles, Luke and Wehner gathered around the map. "Do you have a plan?" Vasconcelles asked.

"I do," Wehner said, taking charge. "I want your flight off first. Frank and I will follow in three minutes. Climb to the base of the clouds and cross the lines headed for Marieulles, Look for Fokkers. If you see any, engage them. If you don't, fly east for five minutes and then come back to Marieulles. Hopefully, by then, we'll have finished our business."

Vasconcelles nodded. It went without saying that if Luke and Wehner had failed to burn the balloon, it would be up to Vasconcelles and his flight to give it a try.

"We'll go in low, just above the fog," Wehner went on. "That way the balloon will be above us and we should be able to spot it against the lighter sky."

"It's set then," Vasconcelles said. "Best not to have more detailed plans when the weather is as chancy as it is today. We'll have a final briefing on the line just before take off."

They each got another cup of coffee and sat down to wait for the rain to let up. Wehner again took two spoonfuls of sugar with his coffee. Luke stared out the window at the rain and the blackness. In an hour, or two at the most, his chance would come. He thought of his mother and father and his brothers and sisters in Phoenix, all probably sound asleep, having no idea of what lay before him. He thought of all the big talk and the bragging he had done on his last leave home. He recognized it now for what it had been. He would set that straight this day. He would set things straight in the squadron as well. In the words of Caesar's mother, he would come home, 'with his shield, or on it.'

The rain gradually let up and it began to grow light outside the window. There was the sound of engines being started and run up. Wehner and Luke walked over to the barracks and changed into their flying clothes. The trees at the end of the field were just becoming visible through the fog. The rumble of the heavy guns that had awoken them continued without let up. On the line, Wehner and Luke's planes had been pushed out beside one another. The mechanics stood by them looking expectantly. This would be no ordinary patrol, not with the guns loaded the way they were, not with the rain still coming and the fog hanging low.

The weather was a long time in clearing. It was past seven o'clock when Vasconcelles walked over to them from where his four aircraft were parked. "As soon as I can see the trees at the end of the field clearly for two minutes, I think we should go. If the fog rolls in while we're up and you can't see the field, just head west. You should have plenty of fuel to find a clear spot where you can land."

Wehner nodded.

"Now remember," Vasconcelles said. "Shoot for the top and hold your guns as steady as you can. You don't want a lot of little holes, you want one big one."

Luke and Wehner nodded. Vasconcelles reached out and shook each of them by the hand. "Good luck," he said and before they could answer he had turned his back and was on his way to his own flight.

Vasconcelles and his pilots buckled into their Spads and the mechanics pulled the props through. The fog swirled across the field and then it cleared. The rain had almost stopped. One by one, the engines came to life. A minute passed and then two and the sky grew brighter. With a startling suddenness, the four Spads came to full power and bumped slowly across the soft ground. They lifted easily and crossed more than a hundred feet over the trees, still in the clear.

Wehner signaled his mechanics and Luke's to run up the engines on their Spads. He took Luke by the arm and walked him to one side where they could stand out of the prop wash. "Frank," he started to speak and then hesitated.

"What is it Joe?" Luke asked, concerned, for Wehner had had a third cup of coffee with sugar. "Is it your head?"

"No, that doesn't matter. This won't be any long patrol. It will all be over in twenty minutes."

"What is it then?" Luke demanded. Behind them they could hear the sound of the engines being warmed up.

"Frank," Wehner said at last. "I'm not afraid to cross the lines or to attack when the odds are against us. I'm not afraid when there are Fokkers above me, or even behind me, because I know that I can give them the slip. But I can't stand to be shot at from the ground by men that I can't see. I found that out the day that McArthur was killed, when Grant and I had to fight our way back across the lines at tree top level."

"I'll lead," Wehner went on. "And I think that we should make the first attack together, side by side, but far enough apart so that they'll have to shoot at one or the other. If we don't get it on the first pass, I know I won't be able to make another. It will all be up to you. I'll stay up and see that no Fokker gets to you, but you'll have to do the dirty work alone."

Stunned for only a moment, Luke slapped Wehner on the back. "All right," he shouted. "All right."

They ran to their waiting Spads and let the mechanics help them into the cockpits. In a minute, they were lifting off and passing over the trees at the end of the field. Visibility ahead was poor, but looking down they could see clearly the neat fields and farms of the French countryside.

Quickly they were over the ugly brown scar of no-man's-land and looking down they could see hundreds and then thousands of men moving across the muddy ground. They searched the sky ahead of them for the shape of a huge cigar.

Wehner saw the balloon first. It was easily a thousand feet above them and no more than a quarter of a mile away. Wehner turned away from it and climbed so that they might attack it from above. As they looked up, there was no sign of Vasconcelles or of any other aircraft. It was probably still raining heavily at the German fields.

They came back around toward the balloon and scattered flashes of light blinked up at them from the dark ground. They had been spotted and were being shot at. They were some three hundred feet above the balloon and Wehner dropped the nose of his Spad to begin the attack. Off to the side and slightly behind, Luke followed.

At full throttle, their speed built quickly. Luke held the stick with both hands and steadied the gunsight against the top of the huge gas bag ahead of them. The balloon loomed ever larger.

Muzzle flashes lit up the ground all around the winch and support trucks on the ground.

They were close enough. Luke pressed both triggers and saw the satisfying sight of tracers arcing out into the semi-darkness and falling into the balloon. Wehner's tracers too, were going home. 'Any second,' Luke thought. 'The whole thing should go up in flames.'

It did not. They pulled up when they were less than a hundred feet away, Luke going to the right and Wehner to the left as they had agreed. As he came around in a wing over, riding right at the edge of a stall, Luke saw two parachutes descending below the balloon. The gas bag itself was intact. Wehner had leveled off above the balloon to the north.

Luke plunged down on the balloon again from almost directly above it. This time there was a solid mass of gun flashes from the ground and streams of flaming onions went flashing across in front of him. He fired again and again the tracers went home. Then, without warning, the right gun stopped and, a second later, the left.

He pulled out of his dive and as he turned away to the east he saw a string of bullets rip through both of the right wings. He climbed clear of the ground fire and turned his attention to the guns. The right he cleared quickly, but the left was jammed with the bolt half open and both an empty and a full cartridge stuck in the breech. He pounded on the bolt with his gloved fist, but he could not move it.

Think. He took a deep breath and scanned the sky around him. Wehner's Spad circled protectively some six hundred feet above him. He reached down in the cockpit and managed to pull off a shoe. He hammered at the bolt of the left gun with the heel and at last saw both cartridges fly out and the bolt slam closed. He cycled two rounds through the gun and then turned his attention back toward the balloon.

They were winching it down as fast as they were able and it was no more than five hundred feet above the ground. He dove to the attack once more and once more the ground turned into an almost solid sheet of flame. He ignored the bullets ripping through the fabric of the wings and poured another long volley of fire into the top of the gigantic shape. He pulled off of his run and looked back to see it still intact and rapidly being lowered to the ground.

He came around quickly and made his next pass almost level,

down the length of the monster. His bullets traced a hundred foot seam down the top of the it and still nothing happened. It seemed to be indestructible. As he pulled away he saw that the right gun had jammed again. A couple of quick pulls on the bolt cleared it. For the fifth time, he rolled back toward the target. In spite of all the fire he had taken, the engine ran smoothly and a quick look at the instruments showed that the temperature and oil and air pressure were all normal. His ammunition, though, was almost gone. It would be his last pass.

The balloon was down to no more than two hundred feet and as he began his firing run he felt the Spad violently shaken as it caught a particularly heavy burst of fire. He waited until he was at point blank range before he fired. One gun quickly ran out and then the other. His wheels passed not more than ten feet above the top of the balloon as he pulled the nose of the Spad up and away.

"God damn it all to Hell!" He slammed his fist against the cowling and buried his head in the cockpit in despair and disgust. He had failed.

Then, as if some great hand had lifted it, his Spad rose a hundred feet and tilted off to one side. Startled, he looked up to see the clouds ahead of him reflecting all the purple and yellow and orange and red and gold of the most spectacular Arizona sunset. Turning to look behind him, he found himself staring into a ball of fire as bright as the sun. He had not failed.

He leveled the wings and looked for Wehner. Off to his right a single Spad came plummeting out of the sky. He turned to the south and Wehner pulled up on his right wing.

Quickly, they were across the brown strip of no-man's-land and once more over the green fields of France. Ahead of them loomed an American observation balloon. Luke reduced power and descended toward it. They came by the balloon low enough to see the men on the ground waving to them. Luke turned and came around into the wind and landed in a field by the balloon.

Wehner circled, wondering what had happened. He saw Luke's propeller stop and Luke get out. Some of the men from the balloon crew ran over toward Luke. Wehner came around again and saw Luke pull off his helmet and goggles and wave them at him. He set a course back for Rembercourt.

When Wehner landed at Rembercourt, confirmation had already come in for the balloon. Before his prop had stopped turning, Grant and Hartney were at the side of the cockpit. "Where's

Luke?" Hartney demanded.

"Down by one of our balloons."

"Hurt?"

"No."

"You sure?"

Wehner nodded. "I circled twice. I saw him cut the switches and get out. The second time I came around he waved to me. His plane could be damaged. You can't imagine the fire that came up on his last passes."

"How many passes did you make?"

"I only made the first one," Wehner said. "After that it was all Frank's show. He made five passes in all. After his second pass, he had to pull off to the side for a couple of minutes to get his guns cleared. They were really waiting for him then."

Wehner pulled himself wearily from the cockpit. By then most of the pilots and mechanics had come up to hear what he had to say.

"You all right?" Grant asked.

"You can't imagine what it looked like," Wehner said, seeming not to have heard Grant. "By the time he made his last pass they had the balloon down to no more than two hundred feet. There were hundred of muzzle flashes coming from all around the winch."

"If it burned that low, he must have got the winch too?" Hartney said.

"Winch, trucks, machine guns, everything. It just fell straight down. It must have killed the whole crew."

One of the operations clerks came running down the line. "Major Hartney, sir," he called out. "We've just heard from an observation post of the Seventh Balloon Company. Lieutenant Luke is down there sir. His plane isn't flyable. They're bringing him with a motorcycle and a side car."

"Well," Hartney said. "I guess I can go and call Colonel Mitchell. Wehner, stick around. As soon as I get my call through and Luke gets back, we'll have a little talk. I want to hear more about this balloon thing. We may have to do another one, one of these days."

Chapter 7

The sky continued to clear and Grant took a flight of six to patrol along the length of the American attack. By then Vasconcelles had returned with his flight of four. They had spotted no Fokkers, but they had seen the glow of the burning balloon. Everyone, the pilots, the mechanics and even the cooks and orderlies waited expectantly for Luke's return.

In a little more than an hour, Luke was back at Rembercourt. The officers all crowded around to hear his story. Even the ones who had been the most sarcastic about Luke's previous claim wanted to hear how it had been done. He gave them little to think about. "I just shot at it until it burned," he said. "Any of you could have done it."

Unspoken, but understood, was the message that they could have done it if they had had the nerve to try. He had taken their sarcasm and snide remarks for two months. He would take it no more. That burning balloon was only a single victory, but the circumstances under which it had been destroyed placed Luke in the first rank of the pilots in the 27th.

The return of his Spad by truck later in the day served only to enhance the image that his victory had created. More than four hundred bullet or shrapnel holes riddled the fabric of the wings and fuselage and tail. A piece was shot out of one of the prop blades and the glass in the compass on the floor of the cockpit was broken. The radiator was holed in two places and the engine block was cracked. A heavy scum of oil covered the entire bottom of the fuselage. By some miracle, the cockpit and the fuel tank beneath the seat were left untouched. All who saw Luke's mortally wounded Spad walked away in amazement, first of all that an airplane in that condition could remain in the air and secondly that any pilot could will himself to face that kind of withering fire for five separate passes.

It was the middle of the afternoon before Grant returned from his patrol and Hartney finished issuing his orders over the field phone. Hartney gathered Luke and Wehner and Grant together in Grant's office and began a critique of Luke's victory that morning.

"First of all," Hartney began. "I should tell you that Colonel Mitchell sends his best regards for a job well done. If the Air Service is ever going to amount to anything, we're going to have to do more command performances like this one. In fact, Colonel Mitchell wants this squadron to concentrate on the development of the capability to pretty much attack and destroy balloons on demand."

Grant swallowed hard to hear that news. It would surely lead to an increase in the number of losses in the squadron. At best, if Luke's airplane was any indication of the strength and accuracy of the ground fire, it would mean late nights for the maintenance crews who would have to patch up the ships. And he had been thinking about working a transfer to the training command at Issouden. Now, with the assignment of this new mission, there would be no chance of leaving.

"First of all," Hartney went on. "What happened that caused the guns to jam? We can't be giving them time to pull the balloons down and get their guns set. We need to get results on the first or second pass. Anything more than that is just plain suicide."

Wehner and Luke looked at each other. Something unseen by Hartney or Grant passed between them and indicated that Wehner should be the one to speak. "As you know," Wehner said. "Six factories in England make ammunition for the Vickers gun. We've been fortunate in getting all of our ammunition from the Vickers factory itself. Even so, my armorer, and Frank's, pass every round through a gauge before it is loaded into the belts."

"I didn't know that," Grant said. "When did all this start?"

"Rickenbacker started it in the 94th when they were getting ammunition from three different factories. Now, most of the armorers do it."

"Doesn't that take a lot of time? And what happens to the rounds that are rejected?" Grant was clearly out of touch with what was going on in his own Squadron.

"They don't find a bad one in a hundred and those are set aside and fired singly when they are sighting in the guns."

"So what happened this morning?" Hartney asked.

"This morning," Wehner said. "We sent down an order to load seven guns with full tracer and seven more with tracer and ball alternated. On such short notice there wasn't time enough to gauge that much tracer. On top of that, the only tracer we had in that kind of quantity was from an American factory. Apparently, the American ammunition isn't up to British standards. Frank was lucky to have only three stoppages."

"We can't have that," Hartney said quickly. "If we have to use American ammunition, perhaps we should switch to the Marlin guns."

"No," Luke spoke for the first time. "That's not the answer because the guns stopping isn't the problem. The problem is that it took us six passes to get it to burn. The thirty caliber incendiary bullets aren't heavy enough and they aren't hot enough to do the job. We need to be able to do the job on the first pass."

"Suggestions?" Hartney asked.

"The French have a forty-five caliber gun that throws a bullet twice the weight of the Vickers," Luke said.

Hartney shook his head. "That gun has been nothing but trouble since the day it was invented. Even the French won't use it. It's the most unreliable weapon on either side of the lines."

"Not the one I shot last week," Luke said.

They all looked at him questioningly.

"The day I was over at the Storks," Luke went on. "They had just received a shipment of the latest modification of the 45 caliber. We shot several hundred rounds through one on the sighting range and didn't have a single malfunction."

Grant looked irritatingly at Luke. He hadn't even known that Luke had left the field except to fly patrols. "So the French think that they have finally improved their 45 caliber gun," Grant said. "What good does that do us?"

"They said I could have two, if I wanted them," Luke said.

Just a minute," Grant said. "You don't have any authority to requisition material from the French, or from any of our own units for that matter. This business has gotten completely out of hand."

"Now wait, Al," Hartney said. "Frank, did they really offer you two of the guns without your asking?"

"Yes sir."

"Well," Hartney paused to think. "It might be worth a try."

"What would we do for ammunition and spare parts?" Grant demanded. "Would our armorers even know how to load them, let alone work on them?"

"They're not so much different from the Vickers guns," Luke said. "If it came to it, I could load and service them myself."

Grant was beat and he knew it. He had not known that Luke had even known of the existence of the French 45, and now Hartney was about to let Luke bring a pair into the squadron. He had only had command of the squadron for a month and already he was loosing control of it to a green horn second lieutenant.

"Frank," Hartney said. "You are going to need a new airplane. Pick out one of the three that came in yesterday and have your armorer pull one of the guns. While they're doing that, I'll call over to the Storks and see if their offer still holds."

"Just one gun?" Luke asked.

"Yes," Hartney said. "There's no guarantee that the 45 won't jam and if you run into Fokkers, you'll want the greater rate of fire that the Vickers gun provides."

Luke started to say something, but a look from Wehner cut him off. "Let's go look at airplanes, Frank," he said. On that note, the meeting broke up.

An hour later, Luke was on his way to the Storks in a new Spad. Before dark, he sent a message that he was spending the night. Shortly after sunset, fog spread over the entire front and flying ceased on both sides of the lines.

Captain Grant worked late into the night, bringing his paper work up to date and scheduling his patrols for the following day. One of the last items in his basket was Luke's combat report.

It read: Took off at 7:30 with Lt. Wehner to attack a balloon near Marieulles. Made five passes, the last with the balloon no more than 200 feet above the ground. Burned the balloon and the supporting equipment. Request confirmation for one balloon.

Grant was about to put it away when he noticed that there was a second piece of paper clipped to the report. It had been folded into a square the size of a pack of cigarettes and, from the stained, worn condition of it, it had to have been carried in a sweaty flying suit for several weeks. It was partly typed and partly hand written in ink. The typing was old and all in capital letters, the writing that filled in the blanks was fresh. It read:

ON _Sept 12, 1918_

AT ABOUT _8:05 hrs_

IN THE VICINITY OF _Marieulles_

I SAW LT. FRANK LUKE DOWN _1_

TYPE _Balloon_

WITNESS _John Snyder_

RANK _1/Lt_

SERIAL NUMBER _100613_

ASSIGNED _7th Balloon Co._

That folded and stained piece of paper made a bad ending for Captain Grant's day. He had about had his fill of Hartney bowing to Luke's every wish and whim. Luke had again managed to get out from under his control. He was at the damned Storks again, doing God only knew what. He could be safely tucked into bed for the night or he could be out carousing at some French whore house. How could he maintain any discipline when Luke could just leave the post whenever he wanted. He was going to have to come down on him, and hard. There would be no privileged pets in his squadron. Every man would toe the mark, just like every other.

Attaching the typed confirmation sheet, signed by the Lieutenant from the Balloon Company, was a deliberate insult on Luke's part. Thousands of men had seen the balloon burn and yet Luke, out of spite, because of Grant's rejection of his first combat report, had risked a landing in a soft field to get the confirmation signed. Luke had not realized how badly his aircraft was damaged until he was down. Grant knew that. He also knew that he would never be able to prove it.

But he would have discipline. By God he would. No refugee from a Wild West Show would be allowed to interfere with the way he ran his squadron. Still, for the moment at least, Luke had Hartney leaning his way. That would change. Luke would trip himself up. His kind always did. Grant had only to give him enough rope and he would find a way to hang himself.

Chapter 8

It was late on the afternoon of the 13th when Luke finally re
turned to Rembercourt with one of the French 45 caliber guns
fitted to his Spad. It had been a cold, windy day with showers from
time to time. Nevertheless, the 27th had put up four combat patrols to escort observation planes across the German lines. There
were heavy concentrations of German troops and artillery immediately behind the lines and the belief was widespread that the
Germans had retreated to draw the Americans into a trap and that
a counter offensive would begin in a day or two.

Fokkers had challenged every crossing of the lines and the 27th
had lost a pilot and a plane without bringing down any of the
Fokkers themselves. The weather to the west was rapidly improv-
ing and it was predicted that the following day would be clear and
warm. Orders came down for every pilot to be dressed and ready
to fly at dawn.

Captain Grant led the first mission, the morning of the 14th.
His flight of four took off while it was still dark and climbed to
12,000 feet where they finally caught the rays of the rising sun.
For an hour they patrolled along the line without catching a glimpse
of another aircraft. From their altitude, they could see no signs of
activity on the dark ground below.

The next patrol was flown by the 94th, and they also saw no
enemy aircraft. By the time they returned, it was after dawn and,
with only a few scattered high clouds, it was apparent that it would
be a perfect flying day. Grant worried over the lack of activity on
the part of the Germans. "They're saving their gasoline for something," he grumbled.

Vasconcelles led a flight of eight to escort a two seater on a low altitude reconnaissance. He returned in less than an hour to report that the two seater had turned back when a large number of Fokkers had appeared some two thousand feet above them. The Fokkers chose not to attack and Vasconcelles was unable to climb to their altitude before they moved off to the east. He had, however, seen a balloon being put up in the vicinity of Boinville where there had never been a balloon before. Apparently, it had been moved in overnight.

The balloon had also been seen by a dozen observers along the line. Hartney had been requested by Mitchell to bring it down and he in turn had given the mission to Grant and the 27th.

When Grant called the pilots together, it was almost nine o'clock. He explained the situation briefly and then he paused and dropped his head almost as if in prayer. Looking up abruptly, he said, "It's a trap. Tactically, it serves no useful purpose. It has been put up deliberately to see if we will go after it the way we did, day before yesterday at St. Mihiel. Only today we will not have the advantage of rain and bad visibility, and we will not catch them by surprise."

"We will try to set a trap of our own," he went on. "I have already talked to Rickenbacker at the 94th and he will lead a flight of eight or ten that will approach as if to attack the balloon at 9:30, but they will stay high and engage any Fokkers that are in the vicinity. We will follow at 10:00 o'clock with every aircraft that we can put up. We will also stay high, out of range of the ground batteries. By that time, some of the Fokkers will be low on fuel or ammunition and Fritz will be putting up some of his reserve. We will have the advantage of altitude on those Fokkers and we will use it. Lieutenants Wehner and Luke will be attached to the last flight. At their discretion, they may at any time attempt an attack on the balloon."

Luke leaned over to Wehner. "What do you think, Joe?" he asked quietly.

"Great plan for us," he said. "But with most of the Spads over the balloon, it leaves the rest of the line open for any German scouts that want to come over and take pictures."

"Questions?" Grant demanded. No one spoke. "Flight line ups will be posted in ten or fifteen minutes. Everyone scheduled, be in your cockpit and be ready to start engines at a quarter of ten."

The meeting broke up and Grant and Vasconcelles began to put together their order of battle. The room was filled with the quiet drone of small discussion. Luke and Wehner went out and started over toward the line to check on their airplanes.

"Didn't think you'd get to shoot your elephant gun so soon, did you?" Wehner said in jest.

Luke shrugged. "I wanted it to use, not to carry for show."

"It does make a good show though, doesn't it," Wehner said as they came up to where their aircraft were parked side by side. The French 45 was both taller and longer than the 30 caliber Vickers gun. It looked like it might bring down an elephant.

Both aircraft had been run up and were ready. Wehner and Luke sat down in the grass and let the warm morning sun beat down on their backs. "We need to talk a little about how we're going to handle this," Wehner said.

"We see the balloon and we go for it," Luke said. "Nothing fancy, no maneuvering for position, just straight down, burn it and home."

Wehner shook his head. "We need to do better than that. We need to stay at altitude, at least for the first go around. We might get some easy chances at some Fokkers. In any case, we want to slip away from the fight without being followed. That's why we should wait until everybody's busy."

"All right," Luke said. "I'll follow. When you think it's safe, dive for the balloon. I'll be right behind you and as soon as we're clear, you can move back and cover my tail."

Wehner nodded. Vasconcelles came down the line chewing on his cigar. "You boys will be tacked on to the end of my flight," he said. "But once you start down, you're on your own."

"If there are a lot of Fokkers, we'll probably stay high," Wehner said.

Vasconcelles grunted and went down the line to where his Spad was parked. The other pilots who were scheduled to fly came out to their planes and talked to their crew chiefs. In all, fourteen aircraft were to be put up, the largest number the 27th had ever flown together.

As it approached a quarter to ten, the pilots began to buckle themselves into their airplanes. Luke and Wehner were among the last to take to their cockpits. There was a nervous checking of watches up and down the line and then Grant's engine turned over and caught and within seconds, all of the other engines were firing. Grant taxied out and the other aircraft sorted themselves out into flights and followed.

Within minutes, they were airborne and climbing for altitude as they crossed the lines. Ahead and above them they could see a mass of dots crisscrossing the sky and a single dot falling and trailing a cloud of black smoke. It looked as if Rickenbacker had found the Fokkers. Soon enough they were close enough to distinguish the Fokkers from the Spads.

Grant, for once, plunged directly into the fight and the flights behind him followed. Wehner slid away from Vasconcelles' flight and into the shadow of a small cloud. For a few seconds he and Luke remained there, hidden from the swirling battle above, and then Wehner plunged directly for the ground.

Luke had been following and at first did not see the balloon. Then, as they half rolled in their descent, he saw the great olive drab shape against the yellow meadow where it was moored. He looked quickly over his shoulder. There were no Fokkers to be seen. They had gotten away clean.

Wehner slowly dropped back and Luke assumed the lead, diving away from the balloon so that he might make his first run right down along the backbone, head to tail. No ground fire came up as he pulled out of his dive and came around toward the balloon. Wehner hung protectively some five hundred feet above him.

The gunsight steadied on the top seam and he fired both guns. The slower firing 45 made a strange coughing sound as it seemed to labor to keep pace with the Vickers gun. But there were no tracers. He could not believe it. He pulled off and came around for another run.

This time the ground lit up with gun flashes and he heard the rip of bullets as they came through the fabric of the wings. Again he fired both guns. This time, every fourth or fifth round from the 45 was a weak incendiary. Against his better judgment he had allowed the Vickers gun to be loaded straight ball. He was ripping long tears in the balloon, but the gas was not burning.

He came around the third time and saw two parachutes descending below the basket. Again the ground fire was heavy and again the tracers burned out before they reached the balloon. The crew was winching it down rapidly. Every pass he made, it was two or three hundred feet lower and he was that much closer to the guns on the ground.

He should have insisted on tracer in the Vickers gun as well as the 45. He had torn almost all of the top seam open and still it was not burning. As he turned in for his sixth pass, the balloon was within a few hundred feet of the ground and he had less than a dozen rounds left in each gun. He waited until the last second and then fired the ammunition that he had left.

The top of the balloon opened up and, although it did not burn, all the gas went out and it fell on the winch and the trucks like a huge tortilla.

Luke climbed away, checking his aircraft for damage. The fabric in the wings was ripped and torn in a dozen places and he knew the fuselage was as well. Oil and air pressure were steady, but the water temperature was rising. He opened the radiator shutters all the way.

He looked around. Wehner was still covering him from above. Off to his left, too far for him to see whether it was a Fokker or a Spad, a plane crashed into no-man's-land and burned. They crossed the lines and were soon making their final turns into Rembercourt. It was just in time. The water temperature indicator was pegged at the top end of the gauge and the engine was beginning to knock. He did not try to taxi in to the line, but shut down the engine as soon as he had come to a stop at the far end of the field.

Luke got out and walked around his Spad. It was torn up almost as bad as the one had been two days before. He could hear the water boiling in the radiator and the engine block. The engine and the airframe each had less than five hours on them and now they were both scrap.

He watched as the rest of the squadron came in to land. But where fourteen had gone out, only twelve returned. He wondered who was missing and how many of the Fokkers they had taken down.

A car came for him and soon they were in the operations room gathered around the table sorting out what had happened. Evans had crashed in no-man's-land. There was no hope that he was alive. Nichols had made it back across the lines and crashed in a hay field. The plane had gone over on its back and it was not known how badly he was hurt.

Vasconcelles and Carrick each claimed victories and several of the pilots reported heavy damage to aircraft. Within minutes, reports came in from observers confirming the victories for Vasconcelles and Carrick and confirming that Luke had indeed destroyed the balloon and the support equipment even though it did not burn. Before lunch, a call came in from a field hospital concerning Nichols. An artillery battery had brought him in in a semiconscious condition with a large gash over his left eye. A dozen stitches had closed the wound and they were now keeping him overnight because of the possibility of a concussion.

In total then, they had lost two aircraft, three, if Luke's was included, and it would never fly again. They had had one pilot killed and another injured. On the other side of the ledger, they had destroyed two Fokkers and killed both pilots and they had destroyed a balloon and damaged the support equipment. As in so many battles, it was difficult to say who had won and who had lost.

Of the most immediate concern to Luke and to Wehner was the ammunition for the 45 caliber gun. It had been marked incendiary, but very few of the rounds had burned, and none had managed to set off a fire in the balloon. Skipping lunch, Luke commandeered a staff car and set off for the Storks to find out what was wrong with the ammunition that the French had given him.

Before he returned, some three hours later, the French Commandant had already phoned Grant to protest Luke's high handed treatment of his supply officer. It seemed that the French had a policy of using their oldest ammunition first, especially when they were giving it away. Luke proposed to change that policy, at least as far as he was concerned, by threatening, to break the supply officer's nose.

One of the supply sergeants had seen trouble coming and had called for the Military Police who had arrived before Luke could make good his threat. But his second threat had been taken more seriously. The French had a store of hand grenades which the pilots sometimes carried to drop on enemy troops. In the confusion involved in the arrival of the Military Police, Luke had gotten hold of one and had pulled the pin. Unless they were ready to see things his way, he informed them, he would throw the grenade into the ammunition bunker and clear out all of their old inventory. The French understood little English, but they had no trouble understanding Luke that afternoon.

The situation was saved by the arrival of Captain Nungesser, at the time the Stork's leading ace. He got the Military Police to lower their rifles and Luke to put the pin back in the grenade. Then he sent for an interpreter and they settled down to the business of what should be done about the ammunition.

They were aware that one of the American pilots had downed a balloon that morning without burning it, but they had not known that Luke had been the pilot and that the ammunition for his 45 caliber gun had been defective.

When Luke described the condition of his Spad when he landed, Nungesser became furious and launched into a tirade that must have made the supply personnel wish they had dealt with Luke. In the end, Nungesser insisted that they carry a dozen or more boxes, of their newest lot, out to the range. The boxes were then opened and sample rounds from each were fired until both Luke and Nungesser were satisfied that there would be no more problems with any of the ammunition.

When Luke returned, the staff car was stacked full of ammunition boxes and additional boxes were tied on to the running boards so that the only way to get in or out of the car was through the window. Grant was waiting.

"Do you know what you have done?" Grant demanded as soon as Luke had managed to climb out of the window.

"Yes Sir," Luke replied. "I have solved the problem of the defective ammunition for my 45 caliber gun and I have got a supply of new and tested ammunition that should last me for some time."

"Did you or did you not threaten to hit the supply officer?"

"I did sir."

"Did you or did you not pull the pin on a grenade and threaten to throw it into an ammunition bunker?" By then a crowd of some size had gathered. Even knowing Luke as they did, this last charge brought raised eyebrows and gasps of astonishment.

"I did pull the pin on a grenade, sir. I may have given them some reason to think I might throw it into the bunker. The door was open. And they don't understand English very well."

Grant stamped his foot in a little fit of temper. Luke had a way of confusing any issue. He should have taken the discussion into the privacy of his office, but he felt compelled to bring Luke down a peg or two in the presence of witnesses.

"Lieutenant Luke, who gave you the authority to act as the representative of this squadron in a transaction with an organization of a foreign government?"

"Well, no one. Except Major Hartney did authorize me to have the French install one of their 45 caliber guns on my Spad."

"But Major Hartney acted as the direct liaison with the French. He personally approved and arranged for the French to give you that gun?"

"Yes sir."

"Then he would also be responsible for the ammunition?"

"No sir."

"Then pray tell who would be." Grant said sarcastically.

"Why, you sir," Luke answered innocently. "This is your squadron. You are responsible for every gallon of gasoline, every round of ammunition, every tin of corned beef, every roll of......" In spite of themselves, many of the officers and men broke out in laughter.

"That's just about enough, Lieutenant," Grant said sternly. "I don't need you, or anyone else, to lecture me on my responsibility as the commander of this squadron. I would suggest that you concentrate on doing your duty and let me do mine."

"With all due respect, sir," Luke said quietly. "I would have you look over beside the second hanger at number twelve." Every eye turned in that direction. "This morning that was a new Spad with less than five hours of flying time. Now it's nothing but scrap. The lower main spar is shattered and the engine is frozen so tight that six men can't pull the prop through."

Luke paused and Grant struggled for something to say, but he had become as fascinated with what Luke had to say as the rest of the crowd that had formed around them.

"This morning's plan was perfect," Luke went on. "When we hit the Fokkers, Joe and I slipped away, under a cloud, and when none of the Fokkers followed, we dove straight for the balloon. They never saw us coming. I made my first pass down the full length of the balloon and there wasn't a single shot came up from the ground. I put over a hundred rounds into it and it didn't burn, because all of the incendiary in the 45 was defective. So I had to make five more passes, every one with the balloon winched down another three hundred feet closer to the guns. And my Spad wasn't the only thing that was lost. If the balloon had burned on my first pass, the way it was supposed to, Joe and I could have climbed back up into the fight. The two of us just might have been able to tip the balance in our favor."

"Well, it's always easy, after the fact to know ." Grant was suddenly at a loss for words.

The orderly saved him. "Major Hartney, on the phone, sir."

Grant went in to his office and picked up the phone.

"Al, Harold here. Did you hear what Luke did over at the Storks?"

"I heard," Grant answered. "From the Commandant himself."

"Doesn't that beat all?" Hartney asked." Nungesser called. I just hung up the phone." Hartney laughed. "Can't you just see the supply officer shitting his pants when Luke pulled the pin on that grenade?"

That was a detail that the Commandant and Luke had neglected to mention and Grant was taken by surprise.

"Nungesser said that he still had a case of the running shits a half hour after Frank was gone. The surgeon had to give him a shot of morphine to calm him down before they could send him home on convalescent leave. Said it was the first case of shell shock he had ever seen in a noncombatant."

"The Commandant didn't think it was so funny," Grant said sourly.

"Oh, hell, he'll get over it," Hartney said. "Will Luke and Wehner be ready to go, later on this evening? We may have a target for them. They're still pretty worried about a counterattack."

"Luke brought back a car full of new ammunition. I'll check right away to see if the guns have been moved to a new airplane." Grant said, suddenly aware of what Luke had said about being responsible for everything.

"New airplane?" Hartney asked. "What's wrong with the one he had this morning?"

"Engine problem," Grant said as casually as he could.

"I see. Well, call in the status as soon as Luke is ready to go." Hartney hung up the phone.

It was almost five o'clock in the afternoon when the call came in reporting the presence of a new balloon near the town of Buzzy. The report also mentioned that Fokkers had been seen patrolling in the vicinity. Grant called in Vasconcelles and Wehner and Luke and together they went over the map. Buzzy was only a short distance across the lines, less than ten minutes flying time from Rembercourt.

"They want that last look before dark," Vasconcelles said. "Clouds are coming in heavy from the west. It will be dark in another hour. If we want it today, we'll have to go soon."

"How soon could you put up eight for cover?" Grant asked.

"Fifteen, twenty minutes at the outside," was Vasconcelles' answer.

"Your airplanes ready?" Grant looked at Wehner and Luke. They nodded.

"Same plan as this morning then?" Grant said.

Vasconcelles shrugged.

"Maybe not," Wehner offered. "It's getting dark fast, on the ground. But the sky will still be light for some time. Our best chance might be for Frank and I to slip across the lines just above the tree tops. That way the Fokkers wouldn't see us, but we could expect to find the balloon against a light sky."

"Your choice," Grant said. He disapproved of the plan, but after what had happened that day, he was wary of challenging either Wehner or Luke.

"Frank?" Wehner asked.

"We'll try it your way," Luke said. "Two of us going in low have a lot less chance of being noticed than eight or ten would going in high."

They quickly calculated the course for Buzzy and noted the check points along the way. At a quarter after five, with the sun already hidden behind heavy clouds, they started engines and taxied out to where they could take off into the wind. A large part of the squadron was down at the line to see them off.

In a matter of minutes they were over the town of Buzzy and looking up at the fat silhouette of the balloon. No Fokkers were anywhere to be seen. They climbed to the east so as to have the lighter western sky behind the balloon for the first attack and they gradually separated as Wehner took his Spad above and behind Luke.

When he was high enough, Luke turned lazily back toward the balloon and began the dive that would carry him into firing range. Again they seemed to have achieved complete surprise as there were no muzzle flashes to be seen from anywhere on the dark ground.

Luke pressed both triggers and tracers arced out from both guns and into the balloon. This time they burned brightly all the way to the target. He pulled out of his dive and into a climbing right hand turn that took him well above the balloon. Looking back over his shoulder, he saw with satisfaction that a small flame was flickering at the tail of the balloon and gradually working its way toward the front. That was more like it.

At that instant, a hail of machine gun fire caught his Spad and he instinctively pulled back on the stick and drove his foot into the right rudder. The plane snapped over to his right and a Fokker passed not twenty feet above his head. He started to turn back to follow the Fokker when out of the corner of his eye he saw another Fokker closing on him from above. There was nothing to do but continue his right turn to attempt to pass below the second Fokker.

Luke's engine stopped without warning and he rolled the Spad inverted so as to pull it into a dive. The second Fokker passed above him and started to turn to follow him down. A glance at the instruments told him that his air pressure was gone.

Where the hell was Wehner? As if in answer, a burning Fokker hurtled down just off his right wing. A second later, a flood of gasoline poured over him and he knew why the engine had quit. The main tank below his seat had been hit.

He rolled upright and switched to the emergency tank and the engine came back on. He looked back over his shoulder. There was another Fokker closing in on him, but directly behind it was Wehner with both guns blazing away. The Fokker suddenly nosed over and plunged vertically toward the ground.

Luke turned toward the lighter sky in the west and put his Spad into a shallow dive. The cockpit was awash in gasoline, his flying suit was soaked and his eyes burned. A spark, any spark, would have turned the airplane into a giant roman candle.

He looked around cautiously. The Fokkers were gone. There was only Wehner above and behind him. They were over the lines and he looked for a place to land, but in the dim light, none seemed suitable. He had to get down somewhere; there was only a gallon of gas in the reserve tank.

Rembercourt appeared directly ahead of him and he made a shallow turn into the wind, closed the throttle, cut the switches and landed. Before the airplane had stopped rolling he had unfastened his seat belt and as it bumped to a stop, he jumped from the cockpit. He stumbled, fell, picked himself up and ran for all he was worth.

Some forty yards from the plane he fell again and did not rise. A dozen men ran out to him. As he heard them coming, he called out, "Don't come near me with a cigarette. I'm soaked with gasoline."

"No Frank." They had him, one man under each arm and they dragged him along to the hanger.

"Get Doctor Holden." "The hose there, turn it on." "Get his flight suit off. His boots too." "Leave his goggles and helmet."

They had Luke's flight suit and boots off and were hosing him down when the surgeon arrived. "Frank, can you hear me?"

"Yes."

"Did you swallow any gasoline? Did you breath in any fumes?"

"No. It's my eyes. They're on fire."

"All right, keep them closed. Let's get him into a shower. Don't have the water too hot."

They quickly carried Luke into the latrine and Captain Holden, the surgeon, pausing only long enough to remove his jacket, took Luke into a shower and proceeded to wash him off with surgical soap. When he had done his hair and face, he carefully removed the goggles and washed around the eyes.

"Now Frank," he said. "Open your right eye. How many fingers?"

"Two."

"Good. Now the left eye."

"Three," Luke said.

"Good. You're not blind. Get him dried off and up to the surgery. I'll be there myself in a minute."

In the surgery, Holden, still soaking wet, sat Luke in the dental chair and leaned him back into a half reclining position. "How do the eyes feel, Frank?"

"They burn."

"Bad? Do you need some morphine?"

"No."

"All right then," Holden said. "I'm going to put a weak solution of cocaine into your eyes. It will take away the burning and let me do an examination."

He put the drops first into one eye and then the other. "Feel better?" he asked in a minute.

Luke nodded.

"Then we'll have a look." He took a pen light and inspected each eye. Then he put some ointment into the eyes and bandaged them. "I can't see a thing wrong," he said. "But we'll keep them bandaged until dinner tonight. You should be in bed, but sitting up. You may get some skin rash from the gasoline. If you do, I can give you something to put on it. If you get sick to your stomach or have trouble breathing, I want to see you right away."

"Thank you doctor. I'll look after him." It was Wehner. "You better get dried off or you'll come down with pneumonia."

Captain Holden nodded. "See you in the mess.

Wehner and Luke sat quietly in their room, the bandages still covering Luke's eyes. They had gone over the flight in detail and understood what had happened. There had been two flights of four Fokkers each and they had been waiting well below the balloon, probably in the treetops, which was why Wehner and Luke had not seen them.

When they had started to climb to attack the balloon, the Fokkers must have seen them against the lighter sky. Using their superior rate of climb, they had closed on Wehner and Luke, but had been too late to prevent Luke's first pass.

Wehner had managed to knock down the leader of one of the flights and scatter the others, but had been unable to reach Luke before the other flight had slipped in behind him as he pulled up from his attack on the balloon. Neither Wehner nor Luke could understand why Luke's Spad had not burned when the gasoline had poured out of the main tank and into the cockpit.

The balloon had burned though. Confirmation for it and for Wehner's two Fokkers had come in from an observation post immediately across the line from Buzzy. The Fokkers were Wehner's fifth and sixth victories and qualified him to have his name entered on the list of allied aces. That should have been the cause for some celebration, but because of Luke's close call and the possibility that still remained of some damage to his eyes or lungs, they were, all things considered, a somber pair.

There was a knock on the door and Wehner stood up and opened it. Lieutenants Lennon and Hoover stood there. One held a bottle of champagne, the other, four glasses. "We'd like to come in, if we may," Lennon said.

"Enter," Wehner said.

"Who is it?" Luke asked.

"Lennon and Hoover," Wehner told him.

"Come in gentlemen. Find yourself seats." Wehner pointed to his bed.

They sat down somewhat awkwardly. Luke could not see, but could only listen to what they said. Hoover finally spoke. "We've come to see if we could make something right that's been wrong for a long time."

"Ordinarily, when a pilot gets his fifth victory, he stands the squadron a party," Lennon went on. "Tonight, we want to change that around. We want to stand a party for the two of you."

"Frank," Hoover said. "We really haven't done what we could

to make you welcome in this squadron, though you'd have to admit that you might not have made your best effort either. With Joe here, we stand guilty as charged. He made every effort to be a part of this squadron, from the very first day we started training in Canada, and we turned our backs on him. Now, we want to change that and make amends as best we can. Frank, we brought a bottle of champagne and four glasses. We hope that the two of you will have a drink with us now and then come over to the mess where the whole squadron can give you a proper welcome."

"We accept," Wehner said before Luke could open his mouth. "Fill the glasses and I'll give the toast."

Lennon and Hoover quickly filled the glasses and one was put into Luke's hand.

"To the best friends I'll ever have," Wehner said solemnly.

"Thank you," Lennon said and they all drank.

The rest of the bottle was poured out and quickly finished. "See you in the mess then in a half hour or so," Hoover said as they went out.

Wehner nodded his agreement.

After the door was closed and they had gone down the hall, Luke said, "Do you really believe that they mean it, after the way they've treated you all this time."

"I do," Wehner answered.

"And did you really mean it about the best friends you'll ever have?"

"I did, Frank. Any man with the courage to just crank up a Spad and fly it across the lines is my brother."

"Even Grant?"

"Yes," Wehner said. "Even Grant, though I'll admit that it takes a certain amount of charity to include him. But think about the others, Frank. You and I are good and we know it. We can fight our way out of trouble, the way we did this afternoon, even when the odds are against us. But most of the others aren't that good. Whatever chance we're taking, they're taking an even bigger one. Your landing this evening, with hardly any light and your eyes burning and the cockpit ankle deep in gasoline, was a better landing than most of the pilots in this, or any other squadron, could make with a good airplane at high noon. If you had flipped over, the way Nichols did this morning, the gasoline would have come pouring down out of the cockpit and on to the hot exhaust stacks and we wouldn't be having this conversation."

Luke was quiet. Obviously thinking.

"Make the most of it, Frank," Wehner went on. "These days won't last for ever. These may not only be the best friends we'll ever have, this may be the best work we'll ever do in our lives."

Luke nodded, still lost in thought. He carefully removed the bandages from his eyes and they began to dress for dinner.

Chapter 9

☆ ☆ ☆

September 15th was another fine flying day with light winds and only high clouds. Wehner flew a patrol in the morning that made no contact with any enemy aircraft. Luke spent the morning in the surgeon's office, having his eyes and his lungs checked. Captain Holden saw only a little redness around the eyes and he released Luke for flying duty in the afternoon.

The afternoon dragged on. Only one patrol of four was sent aloft and it returned in an hour and a half with nothing to report. A little after three o'clock, Major Hartney drove up to the field and he and Captain Grant had a conference in Grant's office.

The pilots were then called in and Hartney explained the purpose of his visit. Pershing and his staff, which included Colonel Mitchell, were still concerned about a counter attack in the vicinity of St. Mihiel. Mitchell had advanced the idea that if they could down enough of the enemy's observation balloons and if they could also keep the enemy's reconnaissance aircraft from coming across the lines, the Germans might be deprived of any information about the distribution of the American forces. If they attacked without adequate intelligence, the Germans themselves might stumble into a trap.

Pershing had immediately approved of the idea and had instructed Mitchell to put it into operation. Rickenbacker's 94th and the French Storks were to be responsible for German scouts coming across the lines. The 27th was to concentrate on downing enemy balloons.

There was a particular balloon at Etain that Pershing and his staff wanted brought down. It commanded a view of one of the main American supply routes and enabled the Germans to keep an accurate count of everything that was sent forward in that area. The moon was almost full and, when the sky was clear, they were able to observe by night as well as by day.

The plan was set the way it had been the previous morning. They were to patrol in force to Etain with Luke and Wehner attached to the last flight. At their discretion, they were to leave the flight and attack the balloon.

The patrol went badly from the start. Ten aircraft started engines, but only seven took off and one of those turned back with some sort of problem before they crossed the lines. Grant was leading and he took the flight to Etain as briefed, but he did not stay around to see if any Fokkers would appear. As soon as they reached the vicinity of the balloon, but before they had actually spotted it, he turned around and headed back to Rembercourt.

Wehner and Luke, with Luke leading, dropped off from the flight and began a slow descending turn to the left that took them around Etain. Grant and the three Spads with him quickly disappeared to the southwest. They had made almost a full circle before Luke spotted the balloon, just off a road to the north of the city. He waved to Wehner and pointed down at the balloon. Wehner waved back and pointed up at six Fokkers some five hundred feet above them.

The balloon would have to wait. Luke advanced the throttle and he and Wehner began to climb up toward the Fokkers. There was no sign of Grant who should have stayed as top cover until he saw the balloon flame. Now he and Wehner would have to deal with the Fokkers against long odds and then, if they had the fuel and ammunition left, they might try for the balloon. It would have been better if he and Wehner had gone alone, just before dark, the way they had the night before.

The Fokkers climbed along with them, shadowing them, but showing no indication that they intended to attack. They were not anxious to take on this pair of Americans, particularly the one who provided the top cover. The night before, a single Spad had slashed through two formations of four, downing two in the process and wounding a third pilot who crashed and burned within sight of his field. This had so unnerved one of the other pilots that he had wrecked his Fokker on landing.

The Fokkers kept climbing and drawing them away from the balloon. Grant and the other Spads were nowhere in sight. They were letting the Germans control the situation. Luke pushed the nose of his Spad down and went for the balloon and Wehner went with him. The Fokkers were slow to react and when they did start down, they were not able to match the speed of the Spads.

Luke was down almost to the level of the balloon and closing on it much faster than he had expected. He had never attacked at such a rate of speed before. Some flaming onions came up, but they all fell away behind him. He concentrated his gunsight on a light colored patch on the nose of the balloon.

He started the guns when he was still a little out of range, held the sight steady, saw flashes of tracers striking all around the white spot and, just as he lifted his sight off of the target and let up on the triggers, he was rewarded by the sight of small flames burning in several places.

He pulled straight up, converting his speed into altitude, and over on to his back. Rolling out level, he saw that Wehner had already turned back into the Fokkers and was engaging them head on. He followed Wehner in and got a good burst into one that was trying to turn on Wehner's tail. The Fokker broke off his attack and Luke let him go to follow Wehner around in a turn to the right.

He tried to account for all the Fokkers. Two were ahead of Wehner and two more were above him. One was diving away to the north, with a thin trail of smoke or steam streaming along behind it. The sixth, although he could not see it, he assumed to be somewhere below and behind him.

As they came around in a right hand turn, he could see the entire balloon burning. They had done their job. They could dive for their own lines and leave the Fokkers behind. But Wehner was not yet ready to give up the game. He had already sent one Fokker home and, to Wehner, two Spads, flown by Lieutenants Luke and Wehner, were more than a match for the remaining five.

Wehner, pulling his Spad in as tight a turn as he dared, was gradually gaining on the two Fokkers ahead of him. Luke, turning equally as tight, was able to stay with him. He still could not account for the missing Fokker.

They passed through a heading of north and were coming around to the east when Wehner, from long range, fired a burst at the two Fokkers ahead of him. At that, they suddenly reversed their turn and dove back toward the north. That was their first and last mistake. Wehner, with Luke following, cut off the corner and closed rapidly on them as the heavier Spads accelerated in the dive.

The two Fokkers above stayed high and the missing Fokker appeared some three of four hundred yards to Luke's rear. The pilots of the two Fokkers in the lead looked back anxiously as Luke and Wehner closed the gap between them, but they made no attempt to turn back to the front lines.

At a distance of some fifty yards, Luke and Wehner opened fire almost simultaneously. Wehner's Fokker immediately, turned over on its back and plunged toward the ground. Luke saw his tracers strike all around the cowling and the cockpit of his Fokker and soon flames were coming out all around the engine. Another short burst brought a flash of fire that sent the Fokker spinning out of control.

Wehner turned back to the right and again Luke followed. The two Fokkers stayed above them and the third continued to follow at what he must have considered a safe distance. Neither Luke nor Wehner were able to understand why the Fokkers had not attacked while they had the advantage of numbers.

They were still not home free. Luke saw that he had no more than a dozen rounds left in the 45 caliber gun and only twenty or so in the Vickers. They were deep in enemy territory. If they should stumble on to any more Fokkers, they might be in for a fight they could not win.

Wehner waved to Luke and pointed out over the windscreen at the front of his Spad. He was having some kind of trouble with his engine or his guns were jammed. Either way, they needed to get back across the lines and down at Rembercourt as quickly as they could. Night was falling. Lights were coming on in the villages and farmhouses below them. In another thirty minutes it would be too dark to see much on the ground.

Luke tried to orient himself. Etain, where he had destroyed the balloon, lay somewhere ahead of them and to his right. Below them was a small town that he took to be Bibinville. And just outside of it, moored almost on the ground, was a balloon.

He had only seconds to decide. The Fokkers were keeping their distance, but they were still in position to attack. Wehner, whatever his problem, could not be expected to be of any help. And, if he fired out all his ammunition at the balloon, he would be unable to support Wehner.

It was too good a chance to pass. He pushed the nose of his Spad over in a dive that was aimed just short of the balloon. A quick look back showed him that Wehner had moved over as if to cover him and the Fokkers were holding their position.

No ground fire came up from around the balloon. Because of the coming darkness, the gun crews had probably all been marched off to supper. Remembering his limited amount of ammunition, Luke picked a spot on the back of the balloon and held his fire until he was at point blank range.

The shots were perfectly placed, ripping long tears in the heavy fabric. As he pulled up from his attack, he was able to look back and see flames spreading along the entire top section of the balloon. He also saw another balloon not a quarter mile away. But there were no more rounds left for either gun and, even if there had been, he had Wehner to think about.

He quickly climbed back up to Wehner's altitude and was concerned when he saw how little power it took to keep up with him. The Fokkers were still there above them. If the Germans could have known that his ammunition was fired out and that Wehner's engine was failing, they would have been cold meat.

It was over almost five minutes before they reached the lines and their escort of Fokkers turned back. Not long after they crossed the American trenches, Wehner's prop stopped dead and he began to descend rapidly. Luke followed him down and watched as Wehner dead sticked his Spad into a pasture full of cows.

Somehow, Wehner managed to miss all the cows and to keep the Spad up on its wheels. Luke circled around the downed airplane and, even in the dim light, was able to see Wehner climb out of the cockpit and wave his arm. Luke set a course for Rembercourt.

When he landed it was almost six o'clock and the sun had set. There was still enough light though if he hurried. Hartney and Grant and most of the other pilots were waiting for him when he taxied up. "Where's Wehner?" was their first question as he shut down the engine.

"Down safe, just over the lines," Luke answered. "We got two balloons and two Fokkers. But there's one more balloon by Bibinville. I need to be refueled and rearmed as soon as possible."

"No," Grant ordered. "It's too late and too dark."

"Sir." It was Corporal Kelly, Luke's crew chief. "You might want to take a look at the airplane."

They all turned and saw oil dripping out of the bottom of the cowling. The entire bottom of the aircraft was smeared with it. There was no chance that it would fly any more that day.

Grant turned away from his examination of Luke's plane. "We've done what we've been asked to do. Let's call it a night and not press our luck. That balloon will still be there in the morning."

"But Captain," Luke protested. "In the morning there will be a full crew manning the antiaircraft guns around it and the sky will be full of Fokkers above it. And in the meantime, with the moon out the way it is, they will have all night to watch our troop movements. Give me another airplane and in ten minutes I'll have that balloon down."

"Out of the question. It's too great a risk."

"It's always too great a risk for you," Luke said bitterly. "It was too great a risk for you to stick around Etain and Joe and I had to take on six Fokkers all by ourselves."

"We never saw any Fokkers," Grant said defensively.

"That's because the minute you got to Etain, you turned tail and ran for home and never looked back."

That stung. And Grant was at a loss for anything to say. Hartney himself had asked Grant why he had brought his flight back when Wehner and Luke were still in enemy territory. Grant's explanation, that the pilots in his flight had had no training in night landings, was somewhat less than convincing.

"Give me an airplane and I'll go back and finish the job tonight," Luke insisted.

"Lieutenant, listen to me," Captain Grant was clearly irritated by Luke's persistence. "This is a military organization and we will have discipline. Now, once and for all, the answer is no."

"Sir," Luke turned this time to Major Hartney. "Colonel Mitchell wanted the balloon down at Etain because it commanded such a good view of one of our main routes to the front. This balloon at Bibinville commands an even better view of that same route. What good is it to bring down one and leave the other?"

There was a sudden silence at the realization that Luke had challenged Grant directly, in front of at least two dozen witnesses.

Hartney looked at the fading light in the west and at the dark horizon to the east. "Do you think you could find it, and find your way back here?"

"Yes sir."

"Al, give him an airplane," Hartney said as casually as he could.

"Airplane?" Grant said, astonished. "I don't know which ones are ready to fly. We haven't posted a status board for tomorrow."

"Give him yours then, unless there's something wrong with it." Hartney commanded.

Grant hesitated, but only for a second. Trained soldier that he was, he knew better than to question a direct order given in the presence of other officers. He would settle the matter with Hartney in private. "Yes sir," he said to Hartney. "Lieutenant," he turned to face Luke. "Decided what you want for ammunition and my armorer will help yours load the guns."

Luke gave Grant and Hartney only a nod and then he was off and running down the line to where Grant's Spad was parked. His crew and Grant's followed and behind them came most of the officers and men of the 27th. In the entire history of the squadron, no one had ever attempted a combat mission with night coming on.

Luke's first orders were for Grant's crew. "Unload the guns and fill the gas tank," he told them. They set to work.

"Do we have two belts of tracer loaded for the Vickers gun?" he asked of his own crew. Smith, his armorer acknowledged that they did and he sent Corporals Kelly and Kline running for them.

"Will we have a problem with chamber sizes with these other guns?" Luke questioned.

"We shouldn't," Smith reassured him. "The two belts that we have are loaded out of all new Vickers factory ammunition that Hartney sent up from Group yesterday."

Kelly and Kline returned with the heavy belts of ammunition and Smith loaded one gun while Grant's armorer attended to the other. By then, Luke had buckled himself into the cockpit. Corporal Kelly handed him a flashlight. "Take this," he told Luke. "You'll need it to read the compass on the way home."

Luke slipped it into his flight suit pocket and signaled for the prop to be pulled through. The engine, still warm, caught quickly and he taxied out away from the hangers and faced the dark line of trees at the end of the field. He had never flown at night. He wondered if there was something that he was forgetting. He would soon find out. He pushed the throttle forward and in a minute was climbing out toward Bibinville into an ever darkening sky.

On a road below, walking toward a light that he could see in the distance, Wehner heard the sound of a Spad engine. Looking up, he saw the familiar silhouette pass above him and disappear into the darkness that was enemy territory. "Jesus Christ, Frank," he cried aloud into the night. "You don't have to win the whole fucking war all by yourself."

Luke passed over no-man's-land, a dark snake that wound irregularly through a landscape where there were the lights of towns and farms on either side. Far to the south he could see occasional flashes as an artillery battery fired from the allied side.

His eyes began to adapt to the dark and the almost full moon came out from behind some clouds. He began to see better all the time.

He reached Bibinville, or at least what he thought was Bibinville, and turned to the east where the balloon was moored. He made two circles above where he thought the balloon ought to be and saw nothing. He had half decided to drop down low and try to find it by looking for it against the moonlit sky and then he decided to give it a few more minutes. Down low, there was always the chance that he might fly directly under the balloon and into the steel mooring cables.

It was peaceful there in the still night air. Grant's Spad was perfectly rigged and the engine ran as smoothly as a sewing machine. There were no gun flashes from the ground. For certain there would be no Fokkers up at that late hour. In the soft moonlight there was no evidence of the ugly scars of war that were so evident in the bright light of day. He took a deep breath and let himself relax.

He imagined that he was home in Arizona, flying over the Superstition Mountains out east of Mesa. What a sight they would be with a full moon lighting the peaks and throwing the valleys into dark shadows. When he was home, he would do it. He would take someone special some night and they would fly over the Superstitions and look down at Weaver's Needle and then follow the Salt River, shining in the moonlight, all the way back to Phoenix. There would be so many places to fly, so much country to explore, so many canyons to scout for Indian ruins.

He widened his circle and kept looking for a large dark shape with smooth edges. He could not know if it would be up high or if they might have heard the sound of his engine and winched it down to the ground. He had the best eyes of anyone he knew. Surely he would find it.

Ten more minutes of looking produced nothing and he was about to ease down to a lower altitude when he saw a flashing light back in the area where he had first started to look. He flew back in that direction, trying to keep his eyes on the spot. The light was no longer flashing, but as he passed overhead he saw, for an instant only, the dark shape that he was looking for. It was well below him.

He reduced power and made a descending turn so as to come

around directly on the reverse of his original course. As he dropped lower he was able to make out the top of the balloon against some moonlit clouds. The balloon was head on to him. He could fire the entire length of it if he needed.

He added a little power and concentrated on holding the sight steady. Without the 45 caliber gun he would need to put his shots into a tight circle. But there was no need to save ammunition. He started firing, holding the sight deliberately on the upper surface of the nose of the balloon. The tracers arced in and struck on a flat angle. Some of them actually skipped off the fabric of the balloon.

When he was too close to hold the sight down any longer, he let the nose come up gradually and continued to fire as he passed down the back of the balloon. He had just started to pull up when there was a flash of light from behind him and the wings of his Spad were suddenly illuminated as if by some giant spot light.

He dove away into the darkness and let it hide him. When he was well clear he got out the flashlight that Kelly had sent with him, shined it down at the compass on the floor and set his course for Rembercourt. While he had the flashlight in his hand, he checked all the other instruments. Everything was in the normal range, the time was almost eight o'clock.

He crossed the lines and began to look for the landmarks that would lead him to Rembercourt. Somehow, nothing seemed familiar. To add to his problems a cloud passed across the face of the moon and, for a time, the ground disappeared entirely. Looking up he could see an even heavier bank of clouds moving in from the west.

He forgot about Rembercourt and let down and started looking for a field where he could set down while he still had the light of the moon. He wanted an empty wheat field or a level patch of cut hay. For sure he didn't want a pasture like the one that Wehner had been forced to take. He didn't care for the idea off hitting a cow at forty miles an hour.

He passed over one field that looked a little short and then he was over some that were even smaller. In a minute or two the clouds would cover the moon. He turned back to the field that had looked a little short. The clouds covered the moon before he reached it.

To the south the fields still lay illuminated by the light of the moon. He turned in that direction. In a minute he was out from under the shadow of the clouds and was once more able to see the ground. He crossed a road, but rejected that as a landing place because of the possibility of telephone poles that he might not be able to see.

Then to his right a long, open field appeared and he cut the power and turned into it. The ground was a long time in coming up and he realized that he was a little fast. He had not been able to tell if there were a fence or a ditch at the end of the field. The dark ground whipped by under him and he hit hard and bounced. He forced himself to hold the stick steady and the heavy Spad settled quickly and this time it stayed down. The ground was rougher than he had imagined and twice the Spad almost went over on its nose.

At last it lurched to a stop and he cut the switches and turned off the fuel. He sat for a moment and then undid the seat belt and stood up on the seat and stretched his arms out on the upper wing and breathed in the cool night air. God, what a night it had turned out to be. First the balloon at Etain and then the Fokker and the first balloon at Bibinville. And then the second balloon at Bibinville, in the dark. That was four victories in something like three hours. He was officially an ace. He had made good on the boast that he had made the day he had come to the squadron. In a day or two his mother and father and his brothers and sisters and all his friends would read about it in the paper. The world, he decided, had not heard the last of Frank Luke.

The clouds drifted across the face of the moon and the entire landscape was thrown into darkness. Unless he wanted to spend the night in the open, he would have to find a farmhouse or a shelter of some sort. He got down from the cockpit and looked the airplane over with the flashlight. It didn't seem to be hurt in any way. The ground, he could see, was a succession of shallow furrows. That was why the landing had been so rough.

He looked all around but could not see a light in any direction. His best bet was probably to walk back to the road that he had flown over. First though, he had to do something with the guns. Loaded as they were, they could be fired by the first kid that came along and pulled the triggers to see what would happen. He didn't want that.

He disconnected the links in the cartridge belts and put the unfired rounds into the cockpit. Then, he cycled each gun through until the chamber was empty. Anyone who knew how to load the guns would have sense enough not to do it. He reached into the cockpit, under the cowling, for his automatic and then remembered that it was in his airplane back at Rembercourt. Well, he didn't expect to need it that night. He started walking toward the road.

Once on the road, he saw a light to the south and started walking toward it. Ten minutes found him at a French farmstead. There was a light in one of the windows and he knocked at the front door. The farmer who answered was in his stocking feet and smoking a clay pipe. Behind him, a woman stood looking out from a hallway.

Neither one spoke English and his French was limited, but they recognized the insignia on his flying suit and they realized that he was an American. The farmer went away for a moment and then came back with a pair of rubber boots in his hand. He put them on and they went out to a shed beside the house.

From inside the shed he produced two bicycles and he indicated that Luke should take the one and follow him. They rode along the road for another five minutes before they came to a small group of houses and what looked like a country store. They were all dark, but the man knocked at the door of the store and soon there were lights and a man who could speak a little English. Luke explained what had happened and asked if anyone had a telephone that he could use to call his squadron.

There was a phone, but of course the owner of the store had to speak to the operator since she spoke no English. There seemed to be no way that they could connect up with the American phone system that served Rembercourt. Then he remembered the Storks and in a few minutes he was speaking to the duty officer, Rene Foucet, who happened to be one of the many French pilots who spoke a little English.

He quickly explained what had happened and asked if Rene could call Rembercourt and let them know that he was down safely. Of course he could and he would also send a car for Luke if he would tell him where he was. Luke put the store owner back on the phone and had him describe exactly where they were. Rene then came back on briefly and said that they would be there to pick him up inside of ten minutes.

When the car arrived to pick Luke up, there were two Storks along with the driver and they had an open bottle of champagne and insisted on a toast to celebrate the newest allied ace. The one Stork made a little speech in French and then the bottle was passed around until it was emptied. Luke noticed a basket on the floor of the back seat of the car that contained several bottles of champagne and he took two out and gave one each to the farmer that had brought him on the bicycle and to the store owner who had made the phone call.

The staff car pulled out headed back for the Storks and left two Frenchmen standing in the road, each with a bottle of champagne in his hand, wondering if the events of the last thirty minutes had really happened.

T he two Frenchmen were not the only ones who were astonished by the events of that evening. On the German side of the line, lights burned and phone operators were kept busy until early in the morning.

The night before, two American Spads had crossed the lines just at dusk, eluded a covering flight of eight Fokkers and burned a balloon at Buzzy. Then, one of the Americans had shot down three of the Fokkers and killed all three of the pilots. Another pilot, landing in the dark, had wrecked a fourth Fokker.

That very night, the two Americans had returned and burned a balloon at Etain, right under the noses of an escorting flight of six Fokkers. When the Fokkers had attacked, the Americans had turned on them and shot down two and sent a third home leaking oil on to a hot manifold and trailing a cloud of smoke. If that were not enough, while the three remaining Fokkers watched helplessly, one of the Americans had made a single pass at a balloon at Bibinville and burned it.

Before all of that news could be passed up and down the chain of command and the blame correctly assessed, a report came in of a second balloon burned at Bibinville at almost eight o'clock at night. The German high command was furious.

One of the American commanders was also not exactly overjoyed at the events of that day. Grant had done Hartney's bidding and let Luke have his plane, but he did not mean to let the incident pass without comment. When Luke had disappeared into the night, he insisted that Hartney accompany him to his quarters.

As soon as the door was closed, Grant came directly to the point. "When you were promoted to command the Group, I was led to believe that the 27th was my squadron."

"It is Al," Hartney said as condescendingly as he could.

"Then, if that's the case," Grant demanded. "Why are my orders directly countermanded and my authority taken away from me in front of my entire officer corps?"

"Your orders weren't countermanded," Hartney tried to reassure him.

"And when Luke asked you for an airplane and you gave him one, after I had just refused him the same request, you say my authority wasn't taken away?"

"Al," Hartney said. "It's a single incident and you're blowing it up out of all proportion."

"By God, I am not," Grant insisted. "I'm not commanding the James Gang or Pancho Villa's Irregulars. This is the United States Army and we are fighting a war, not some hillbilly, backwoods feud. We can't have our officers threatening officers of an allied force with hand grenades. We must have discipline. And if we can't have it on the ground, how in the hell will we ever have it in the air? How can you expect me to accomplish anything if you won't back me up?"

Hartney thought for a time. "I suppose you are right," he said finally. "But Al, sometimes when a boy wants to go and fight, you have to let him do it, that or break his spirit. I've seen men with their spirits broken who, when they were ordered to fight, wouldn't do it. It's not a pretty sight. I don't think that you want anything like that to get started in your squadron."

"But no one has ever attacked a balloon at night," Grant countered. "It's a suicide mission."

"Seems to me that Luke is the one that decided to take the risk. He's the only one that has anything to lose. The government will always buy you another airplane."

"That's the point," Grant insisted. "That's the point exactly. Any minute now, the phone in operations will ring and some artillery observer will report a balloon burning over Bibinville. And then in a few more minutes Luke will be back, cockier than ever. Luke isn't going to lose anything. But for every balloon that he burns on these midnight raids, we're going to lose a hundred other pilots who are going to try to do the same thing and who are going to find out, when it's too late, that they don't have either his luck or his skill."

"You really believe that?" Hartney said.

"I've seen his kind before," Grant said. "Always the instigator of some wild scheme or other, but it always happens that one of the followers is the one that gets hurt. You'll see. He'll come out of this war a big ace and go back to Arizona and be elected Governor and then to the Senate where he'll be the leading authority on military aviation and preside over military appropriations for twenty years or more. He'll die in bed at age ninety, surrounded by dozens of adoring children and grandchildren. But I'll tell you, as sure as God made little green apples, that you'll be able to fill a good sized cemetery with the pilots who are killed trying to be like him."

Hartney had no answer for Grant. Pursuit pilots such as Luke and Wehner he understood to be somehow a different breed of cat, not subject to the ordinary kinds of military discipline. But there was no way to explain that to Captain Grant, at least not that night.

There was a knock on the door and when Grant asked what it was, the orderly said simply, "Sir, we've had a report of a balloon burning east of Bibinville."

Hartney got up to leave. "I've got to be on my way," he said. "Have someone call my headquarters when Luke is down."

Grant held the door open for him as he went out. Both realized that absolutely nothing had been settled.

Chapter 10

Daylight was fading fast and the little group gathered on the elevated platform that served as the control tower at Rembercourt looked alternately at their watches and at the road that led into the field. Out on the field, two Spads had been pushed out of the line and turned into the wind. The engines had been warmed up and then shut down and the pilots waited impatiently for a signal from the tower to restart and to take off.

At last, a few minutes after seven o'clock, a heavy black sedan turned onto the service road and bumped its way slowly toward the flight line. "Are you certain that it is Colonel Mitchell?" Hartney asked the sergeant with the field glasses.

"Yes sir. I can make out the flying service emblem on the bumper."

Hartney leaned over the railing and swung his arm in a circle and almost immediately the two Hispano Suizas barked into life. The car pulled up alongside the tower and the driver opened the door for Colonel Mitchell. Hartney waved his arm forward and the two Spads came to full power and started their take off run. By the time Colonel Mitchell and an older man in civilian clothes had reached the top of the stairs, the Spads had crossed the trees at the end of the field and taken a heading for the front lines.

"What's going on?" Mitchell asked, looking toward the Spads that were disappearing into the twilight gloom.

"Just a little entertainment we planned when we found out that you were coming to pay us a visit," was Hartney's answer.

The news of Luke's three balloons and a Fokker and Wehner's Fokker the evening before had not taken long to reach Mitchell's headquarters. The two Fokkers could not be confirmed because they had been shot down at a low altitude, deep in enemy territory, but no one doubted for a moment the validity of the claims. Luke's three balloons though, had all been confirmed and he and Wehner stood even with six confirmed victories each. Colonel Mitchell had come to dine with the 27th and pay tribute to his two newest aces.

Introductions were made all around. Beside the two signalmen on the tower, there were Major Hartney, Captain Grant and Captain Rickenbacker who had come over from the 94th at Mitchell's request. With Colonel Mitchell was Jay Harrison, a writer from the New York Times.

"Just when does the entertainment begin?" Mitchell asked. He was in an expansive mood. His pursuit squadrons had scored heavily in last few days and, that morning, he had been given authorization to go ahead with the planning of a bombing raid on Germany.

In response to Mitchell's question, Hartney consulted his watch and said, "In exactly four minutes and thirty seconds."

"What kind of entertainment are we to have?" asked Harrison, the corespondent from the New York Times.

In answer, Hartney gave him a pair of field glasses and instructed him to look at the eastern horizon at a point between two groves of trees. Hartney, watch in hand, continued with his time keeping.

The minutes passed in silence with everyone's attention focused on the eastern horizon. Finally, Hartney said, "Any second now."

At the instant he spoke, a glow of light appeared between the two groves of trees. "Number one," Hartney said as the glow grew brighter and there was a cheer from the officers and men gathered at the foot of the tower.

"My God, what is that?" the correspondent asked.

"Balloon burning at Reville."

In less than a minute there was another glow on the horizon to the left of the first. "Number two," Hartney said and again there was a cheer.

Ten seconds later, there was a glow to the right of the first. "Number three?" Hartney said questioningly. There had only been two balloons reported in the vicinity of Reville. A roar went up from the officers and men. There was no question in their minds.

"Take a good look at that," said Rickenbacker in a tone of stunned amazement. "You'll never see anything like that again in this war. That's got to be the greatest piece of flying ever done."

The others watched in silence as the fires burned brighter and then gradually began to fade. Hartney, still keeping the time, called for flares. In an instant a green one went up and it was quickly followed by two red ones.

"It's a signal for Luke and Wehner," Hartney explained to the correspondent. "We found out last night that the field can be hard to find in the dark. If they are having any kind of trouble, we don't want them to have to search for it."

The correspondent nodded.

"Flares," Hartney said again and, again, a single green was followed by two reds.

From the east there came the sound of aircraft engines approaching. "Light the pots," Hartney ordered.

The order was passed and out on the field two men ran along lighting oil pots on each side of the landing boundary. At the end of the field, all the automobiles available, including Mitchell's staff car, turned their headlights on to the landing area.

"Flares once more, please," Hartney asked. As soon as he spoke, it was done.

The rough staccato of the throttled back engines could be heard clearly and soon two dark shapes passed across the face of the moon. They turned in the half light like two ghostly images and dropped down into the brightly lit landing area. In less than a minute they were taxiing back toward the main hanger.

The engines were shut down and the planes, with Luke and Wehner still in the cockpits, were quickly pushed inside and the hanger doors closed. The crowd of officers and men that had swarmed around the two planes, parted to let Colonel Mitchell and the rest of the party up to where Luke and Wehner stood.

"What happened?" Hartney wanted to know. "There were only two balloons sighted this afternoon."

"They could have missed one, or they might have brought the third in just before dark," Wehner said.

"Fokkers?" was Hatney's next question.

"None," was Wehner's reply. "They must have gone home before we got there or they just didn't see us until it was too late."

"Who did the shooting?" Mitchell asked.

"We went in like always with Frank leading and me following and watching for Fokkers," Wehner said. "Frank couldn't have fired more than twenty rounds before the balloon went and we pulled up in a climbing left turn to go for the second one. Then, out of the corner of my eye, I saw this third balloon to my right. There were no Fokkers in sight, and my guns were loaded full incendiary, so I went for it. Both flamed on the first pass and we turned for home."

"Ground fire heavy?" It was Rickenbacker.

"Like the Fourth of July," Luke said. "I wouldn't have wanted to make many more passes."

Colonel Mitchell poked at some bullet holes in the rudder of Luke's Spad with the riding crop he carried and a piece of fabric the size of a dinner plate fell off. The others began to look carefully at the two planes. Bullet and shrapnel holes were everywhere. The propellers and the engines though, seemed to be untouched.

"You boys should take better care of these airplanes," Mitchell said smiling. "They cost the taxpayers more than ten thousand dollars each."

"I hear balloons go for a hundred thousand," Rickenbacker said.

"They do for a fact," Mitchell said. "If you include the ground support equipment."

"And these Spads aren't exactly write offs," Hartney said.

"Surely they won't fly again," Mitchell said.

"Probably not, but the engines look to be all right and the guns certainly are," Hartney said. "We'll also salvage the instruments and the controls. They're far from a total loss."

"Well," Mitchell put his arms around Luke's and Wehner's shoulders and started them toward the door. "It's the two of you that can't be replaced. We can always get the French to build us a few more Spads, but you two boys are something else again. I want you to look after each other."

The group of Mitchell and Luke and Wehner followed by Hartney and Rickenbacker and the New York Times correspondent passed out of the hanger and into the now dark night. Captain Grant followed along behind. It was his squadron and they were his pilots, but no one had bothered to speak to him or to even acknowledge his presence.

The slight to Grant was repeated at the dinner that night that Colonel Mitchell gave for Wehner and Luke. Though he had been seated at the head table, Grant was introduced only as the commander of the 27th Pursuit Squadron. Then Mitchell had gotten Rickenbacker and Hartney and Wehner and Luke on their feet together and introduced them as his four aces. At that, the other officers had roared. They had roared again when Mitchell told them that they could all have the next day off. It seemed that a storm was moving in off the channel and that they would wake to a day of high winds and rain.

The spirits flowed freely after that. Confirmations had come in quickly for the three balloons and, of the American pilots active on the front, Wehner with seven victories and Luke with eight, stood behind only the great Rickenbacker himself.

When Colonel Mitchell left it was almost midnight and the party was still in full swing. Hartney and Grant saw him to his car. As Mitchell had said, a storm was moving in from the channel. The wind had come up, clouds hid the moon and rain was beginning to spit down.

"Tomorrow will be a good day to catch up on paper work," Mitchell said. "And two pieces of paper that I want to see on my desk by the end of the day are Distinguished Service Medal recommendations for those boys. You start them Captain. You endorse them Major and get them up to my headquarters. You have no idea what those two have done for the credibility of the Air Service. I mean to see that they get their due recognition."

Chapter 11

The pilots of the 27th Squadron woke to the sound of rain hammering against the windows. Most, pulled the covers up and rolled over and went back to sleep. Not until noon did they begin to straggle over to the mess in small groups for coffee and something to eat. Luke and Wehner were some of the last to splash their way across the board planking that led to the mess. Luke noted that Wehner took several cups of coffee with sugar. It had though, been some night. Wehner was far from the only one nursing a headache.

The afternoon dragged on. A few of the pilots started a game of pool and a couple of card games developed, but the majority drifted back toward the barracks. Luke and Wehner were in that group. Both had letters that they wanted to write.

For Captain Grant though, the 17th was not a day of rest. As Mitchell had told him, and Hartney, it would be a good day to catch up on paper work. Always meticulous in his record keeping, Grant took the opportunity to bring all of his reports up to date. It was late in the afternoon before he had finished the last of them and then an envelope with the return address of the New York Times was delivered to his office. It was their foreign corespondent Harrison's article on Luke and Wehner sent to him for censorship and approval. It was datelined September 16th, An American airfield at the front in France by, Jay Harrison, Special Correspondent for the New York Times. Grant read without much enthusiasm.

AMERICAN ACES STRIKE TERROR
INTO GERMAN BALLOON CORPS

It is seldom, when one is invited to a party, that the guests of honor are expected to provide the entertainment. I had the privilege of attending such a party this evening at one of our airfields just behind the lines.

At shortly after 7 PM, I stood on a raised observation platform and watched two Spads take off, turn toward the front and quickly disappear into the gloom of the oncoming night. With me on the platform were Colonel William Mitchell, Commander U.S. Air Service in France, Major Harold Hartney, Canadian Ace and Commander of the 1st Pursuit Group, Captain Alfred Grant, Commander of the 27th Pursuit Squadron, and Captain Edward Rickenbacker, Commander of the 94th Pursuit Squadron and, with 9 confirmed victories, America's Ace of Aces.

We had not long to wait for the entertainment to begin. Exactly five minutes later, with Major Hartney calling the shot to the second, an orange glow appeared on the eastern horizon. Hartney informed us that it was a German observation balloon burning over Reville. The glow grew brighter and larger and then, no more than a minute later, a second glow appeared to the left of the first. Seconds later a glow to the right of the first announced the death of a third German balloon.

For several minutes all three balloons burned brightly on the eastern horizon. In all probability, this spectacle was witnessed by tens of thousands of troops on both sides of the lines. Imagine if you can, the effect of this on the moral of the German troops. Imagine its effect on the American troops to see two of their own flyers venture so insolently across the lines and strike the Boche three such lightning blows.

Its effect was certainly not lost on Captain Rickenbacker who was the first among us to manage to speak. He proclaimed in awed admiration that it was the greatest demonstration of flying that he had ever seen. And yet, we had seen no flying demonstration at all, only its deadly result. It was Rickenbacker's experience and imagination that allowed him to visualize what must have taken place.

Soon enough we were to have the story first hand. Flares were sent up and, in a matter of minutes, we heard the sound of aircraft approaching. With only the light of the moon and that of a half dozen automobile headlights to guide them, the two Spads glided down out of the dark sky and on to their designated landing area. Scarcely a quarter of an hour had elapsed since they had launched themselves into the gathering darkness. And yet, in that short space of time, they had destroyed over a quarter of a million dollars worth of German equipment.

In a hanger where the aircraft were quickly pushed by dozens of willing hands we met the two newest aces in the U.S. Air Service. They are Frank Luke Jr. of Phoenix, Arizona and Joe Wehner of Boston, Massachusetts. Since the beginning of the St. Mihiel offensive, less than a week ago, these two aviators have been officially credited with nine German balloons and two of the newest model Fokker pursuits. An additional two Fokkers were shot down deep in enemy territory and at a low altitude and so could not be confirmed by ground observers on the allied side of the lines.

German balloons, Colonel Mitchell explained, are extremely difficult to attack as they are usually protected by patrols of Fokkers above and nests of machine and antiaircraft guns on the ground. As evidence of the gauntlet of fire that every aviator must run in order to attack a balloon, Mitchell pointed out dozens of holes in both Luke's and Wehner's Spads. Neither Luke nor Wehner expressed much concern over the damage done to their machines. Both, I was told, had previously returned in much more seriously damaged aircraft.

After the dinner given in their honor, I had the opportunity to talk with both of these boys. I wish every American could have been there with me and looked into the laughing eyes of these two terrors of the German Observation Balloon Corps and shared with me the profound pride that I took in the fact that such men were flying planes bearing the American insignia. The two are a study in contrasts. Wehner, a tall, dark haired, handsome boy of 23, has all the polish and social poise that one would expect of an Ivy League graduate who has traveled extensively abroad. Luke, blonde and blue eyed and only 20 years of age, is a self assured Westerner who has hunted and prospected all across his native state of Arizona from the Grand Canyon to the Mexican border. He is exactly the type of outdoorsman that President Roosevelt recruited when he put together the Rough Riders to serve in the Spanish American War.

In spite of these differences, they have combined to make themselves the deadliest pair of balloon busters in the history of the war. Since the opening day of the battle for St. Mihiel, they have never failed to destroy at least one balloon on every combat patrol that they have flown. Luke's confirmed victories now stand at eight; Wehner, with seven, is only one behind. If they can continue to score at anywhere near the rate that they have set this last week, one or the other is destined to soon become America's Ace of Aces.

When America entered the war there was some question as to whether her untested, raw recruits could stand up to battle hardened German veterans. That question was answered by the Marines at Bellau Wood and by the Army at the Argonne Forest and at Chateau Thierry. It is now being answered by the Air Service in the skies over St. Mihiel by pilots such as Luke and Wehner and Rickenbacker.

Every day brings increasing evidence that the Star Spangled Banner does indeed wave not only Over the Land of the Free, but The Home of the Brave as well. Americans, and indeed the world at large, might do well to stop and consider the way in which the sons of immigrants have been molded into a military force that, by the end of the war, will make the United

States the most powerful nation ever to exist on the face of the earth.

                                                        End.

Clipped to the typed article was a note in Major Hartney's hand. It said: 'Great publicity for the Air Service, but don't think we should clear for security reasons. Let the Germans figure out for themselves what's happening to their balloons.'

Grant wrote out below Hartney's note: Agree and his initials A G. and marked the envelope for return to Group Headquarters.

But he did not agree. He thought that none of it should ever be released. He did not believe that you should set any individual up as more important than the group at large. Luke was already difficult enough to manage. If a story like that appeared in the papers, he would be impossible to control. Team effort was what it took to win ball games, and wars.

Two more sheets of paper remained in Grant's in basket. They were the carbon copies of the recommendations for Distinguished Service Medals for Wehner and Luke that he had sent up to Hartney that morning. If anything, they aroused in him a sense of unfairness even greater than the article by the New York Times correspondent.

The recommendations would be approved. Colonel Mitchell would see to that. And there would be one for Rickenbacker and for Hartney too. As far as he knew, they could already be in process. But there was no medal for Alfred Grant. And he had worked harder than all of them trying to make a combat unit out of the 27th. Rickenbacker had been lucky. He had inherited all of the pilots from the Lafayette Escadrille and had experienced men to spot around among the new replacements.

Grant filed the documents away. Others were always taking away what should be his because they would not obey orders. That terrible mission in July when they had escorted the two seater north of Chateau Thierry. McArthur had disobeyed his order to maintain formation and withdraw and had stayed to protect the two seater. A gallant gesture, but a futile one. With so many Fokkers against them, the two seater was doomed from the start. If all eight of them had stuck together they all might have made it back across the lines. As it was, only he and Wehner had landed safely. Two out of eight. Nothing had ever been said directly, but he knew that everyone blamed him. And it had all been McArthur's fault for not obeying orders.

Now it was starting again with Luke. Going over his head directly to Hartney to get his airplane when he had already refused it. All the time he was spending with the Storks. Threatening their supply officer with a hand grenade. Questioning his turning back with the covering flight from Etain when there hadn't been a Fokker in sight. He was going to have to get a leash on Luke and soon. That or kiss his whole military career good-by.

Promotions would be hard to come by in peace time, but there would be advancements for good staff officers, like himself, who could take responsibility. If Colonel Mitchell had his way, the Air Service would be rebuilt from the ground up; new airplanes, new tactics, new facilities. He wanted to be a part of all of that, but the opportunity would not come to him if he was unable to maintain control of his own squadron.

He saw the situation clearly. The Germans were not the enemy. It was Luke and the others like him who would not accept military discipline; they were the real enemy. If Luke wanted a fight, he would give him one. But it would be on his terms and at a time and a place of his choosing. That boy would know something about the Army when Captain Alfred Grant was finished with him. He promised himself that.

Chapter 12

☆ ☆ ☆

By the morning of the 18th, the rain had stopped and the sky was beginning to clear. There were soft spots on the field, but these were quickly marked with flags and operations began shortly after first light. If the Germans were to launch a counter attack, it would have to be that day or the next. After that, the American troops would be too well established in their new positions and the reserves would have come up.

Orders came down from Group Headquarters holding Luke and Wehner on the ground with their aircraft ready to take off on five minutes notice. If any balloons were put up that day, they were to be brought down as quickly as possible.

The day wore on without any serious action being reported anywhere along the line. German Fokkers and two seaters were seen, but they always withdrew when approached. There was little action on the ground. It was still not known whether the Germans had decided to forfeit the ground they had lost or whether they were gathering themselves for an attack.

At a little after three, a call came down from Group Headquarters. Two German balloons had been put up just across the line at Labeauville and the German artillery had begun to fire in a ranging pattern on the weakest section of the American line.

Hartney spoke to both Grant and Vasconcelles. Colonel Mitchell wanted the balloons down as soon as possible, but he suspected that the Fokkers would be out in force and he wanted a covering flight of at least a dozen Spads.

The front line map was soon spread out over the operations table and the positions of the balloons plotted. Vasconcelles, setting the order for the covering flight, quickly realized that he would be short of aircraft and called over to the 94th for reinforcements. When Rickenbacker heard what was afoot he told Vasconcelles that he would personally lead a flight of four and be at Rembercourt in less than ten minutes.

Wehner took Luke outside where they could look at the sky. There were still a lot of scattered clouds left from the night before. "What do you think, Frank?" Wehner asked.

Luke shrugged. "If the Fokkers show in any kind of numbers, no plan of ours will hold up for more than thirty seconds. If Grant leads the covering flight, that's about how long it will take him to turn for home."

"Rather try it with just the two of us?" Wehner offered. "We could sneak over just at the base of the clouds. That would make it hard for the Fokkers to spot us from above and anything below us would be easy pickings."

"What about the covering flight?"

"They can cross the lines above the first bunch of clouds," Wehner said. "The Fokkers will think twice before they let that many Spads get much of an altitude advantage on them."

"Could we perhaps get this patrol off before dark?" Vasconcelles had come down the steps from the operations office.

Wehner explained to him what they had been talking about. Vasconcelles thought for a moment. "Might be the best thing." he said. "Big formations have a way of attracting a lot of attention."

Vasconcelles went in to talk with Grant. Rickenbacker and three other Spads from the 94th landed and taxied back up to the hangers. The hat in the ring emblem was distinct on the side of each aircraft.

The tension began to build as Spad after Spad was armed and pushed out on to the line. Rickenbacker went in to operations to confer with Vasconcelles and Grant.

The order of battle was set. Grant would lead the first four. Rickenbacker's four would come next and behind them, four led by Lieutenant Coleman. Vasconcelles and Lieutenant Chapin would trail the formation as decoys, acting as if they were the ones designated to make the attack on the balloons. Luke and Wehner were to leave three minutes after the others and make their attack independently.

The pilots scattered along the line to where their planes were parked and soon there was sound of one engine after another being started. In a minute all fourteen were running and they began to move into position. The wind was strong out of the northwest which meant that they had to taxi across the field before they could begin their take off run. Mechanics ran along at the wing tips of each plane to ensure that they did not taxi into one another and to see that they missed the soft spots on the field.

As Wehner and Luke watched, the flights took off and made a climbing turn to the left that took them around the field and away from the front. They would not attempt to cross the lines until they had gained enough altitude to be well above the first layer of clouds.

"Pretty sight," Wehner noted as the fourteen Spads passed across in front of a puffy, white bank of clouds. Luke nodded, but only out of politeness. He was anxious to get on with the day's business.

"Look Frank," Wehner said abruptly. "Let me lead. I don't want you to have to think about anything but the balloons."

Luke nodded his approval. It was Wehner's plan. If anyone could set him up in perfect position to attack the balloons, it was him.

"Now, one more thing," Wehner said as they stood behind their Spads. "Stay close to me, not more than a wing span away. If we run into a lot of Fokkers, I may want to duck into a cloud and I want you with me. If there are Fokkers down below the clouds, we'll go for them. The balloons will still be there later on this evening."

"All right."

They climbed into their cockpits and buckled in. It was exactly three minutes since the others had taxied out. Both engines had been warmed up and they started on the first try. In less than a minute they were airborne and climbing for the base of the clouds.

They crossed the German lines at three thousand feet and drew a few scattered bursts of anti aircraft fire. The air was clear and visibility forward and down was good. There were only scattered breaks in the clouds though and they could see very little above them. By the same token, it would be difficult for anyone above the clouds to see them. Luke concentrated on keeping an eye out for Fokkers and left the navigating to Wehner.

They were some distance into enemy territory before Wehner turned to the southeast in the direction of the balloons. At every break in the clouds above them, Wehner and Luke searched for enemy or friendly aircraft. They saw nothing.

They were still tight up against the bottom of the clouds when Wehner pointed at the ground just ahead and to their right. Two balloons hung there less than a thousand feet below them. They were, at the most, a half mile apart. Luke nodded. Wehner pointed down again and gave him the thumbs up signal.

Luke put the stick forward and pointed his Spad short of the first balloon. His speed increased quickly and soon the wind was screaming in the bracing wires. No muzzle flashes showed on the ground. He wondered if he had been seen at all.

Level with the balloon, but still out of range, he pulled his Spad up and settled the gun sight on a spot where two seams in the fabric crossed. Just as he reached for the triggers, he saw the first muzzle flash from the ground. Wehner's approach from the German side of the front had caught them completely by surprise. It was going to be easy.

One short burst split open the top seam and started a tongue of flame a yard long working toward the rear of the balloon. He turned away so as to avoid the flash, if there should be one, and looked for his second target. Its crew had been more alert. The observer was already drifting toward the ground in a parachute and the balloon was being winched down to the ground. A quick check above him showed Wehner still holding tight against the clouds overhead. A string of flaming onions passed behind him and a short burst of machine gun fire ripped through both of his left wings. He turned hard to the right and back again to the left.

The second balloon loomed ahead of him. He steeled himself for the hail of ground fire that was sure to come. He had not long to wait. One string after another of flaming onions rose up to greet him. He skidded the Spad, from one side to the other as the tracers from the machine guns flashed by on all sides of him. Then it was time to fire.

He centered the rudder and laid the sight dead on the top edge of the balloon. Bullets ripped and tore at the fabric of the Spad, but he shut out everything but the gun sight and the broad back of the balloon.

He pulled the triggers on both guns and the tracers slanted into the huge gas bag at a perfect angle. In seconds, it was all aglow along the top and he was pulling up and away. Off his left wing, a burning Fokker plunged almost vertically toward the ground. Looking up he saw Wehner turning hard on to the tail of another Fokker and behind Wehner four or five more Fokkers dropping down through a hole in the clouds.

He had hardly started to climb to help Wehner when two more

Fokkers dropped through the clouds and dove for him. They were two against one and they had the advantage of altitude and position. Their speed built quickly as the angle of their dive increased and they rapidly closed the distance between themselves and Luke. Discretion and every rule of combat dictated that he should dive away toward his own lines. Instead, Luke jammed the left rudder to the stop, laid the stick full over to the left and bottomed it back against the seat. The Spad reared up and snapped over in a half roll that left it facing head on to the approaching Fokkers.

Luke leveled his Spad and brought his guns to bear on the leader. As he reached for the triggers, the muzzles of the Fokker's Spandaus were already flashing and he could hear the bullets ripping through his upper wing and whistling over his head. His own tracers went dead into the Fokker and the muzzle flashes stopped. When they were only yards apart, the Fokker suddenly tipped forward and passed beneath him.

The second Fokker, a hundred yards behind the first, tried to pull up and out of Luke's way. Luke rolled his Spad to cover him and, as the Fokker passed overhead, he pulled the nose of his Spad up and ahead of the Fokker. Then, with the nose of his Spad completely blanking out the Fokker, he started the guns running.

The Spad shuttered as it began to stall and the Fokker passed not thirty feet above it and directly through the stream of his tracers. The Spad snapped off on the right wing and the nose fell through the horizon. Full left rudder and forward stick steadied it and the airspeed began to build. Luke looked back for more Fokkers coming down out of the clouds, but there were none.

Behind him he could see the two balloons burning in the air and, spaced out ahead of them, his two Fokkers trailing clouds of thick black smoke as they fell, out of control. Ahead of him, where he had last seen Wehner, there was nothing but clouds and empty sky. He pushed the throttle forward to climb up into the fight that must be raging above the clouds. As the RPMs reached 1600, the engine began to shake violently and then, abruptly, it quit.

He quickly scanned the gauges and saw that the air pressure was at zero. A few quick strokes on the hand pump brought the pressure up to twenty pounds and the engine caught again, but it still ran rough. He switched from one magneto to the other, but it made no difference. The engine quit again and once again caught when he brought the air pressure up with the hand pump. That was good. It was the engine driven air pump that had been hit.

The main tank itself, below the seat, was intact and he was not leaking gasoline.

He continued working the hand pump and brought the tank pressure up to forty pounds. With the engine shaking the way it was there was no longer any hope of his climbing up to help Wehner. His main concern was to gain the thousand feet or so between him and the base of the clouds so that he would have some cover crossing the lines.

The Spad was heavy on the controls and needed left rudder to keep from yawing to the right. It climbed reluctantly with the engine turning only 1600 RPMs. If any Fokkers showed up, he would be a sitting duck. He wished that he had Wehner three or four hundred feet above him.

The air was cold, but he was soon sweating heavily from the effort involved in working the hand pump and from the strain of constantly looking around him for enemy aircraft. The wind from the northwest was strong and, in spite of his crab into it, he was drifting south along the line into the French sector.

After some five minutes he had gained the altitude he needed to put himself into the bottom edge of the overhanging clouds. He turned west then to cross the lines. He was too far downwind to make it back to Rembercourt, but there was a chance that he might reach the Storks. There was a large hole in the clouds just as he crossed no-man's-land. When he looked above him, there were no other aircraft in sight.

Ahead of him though, he could see three aircraft at about his altitude. If he continued on his heading, he would pass quite close to them. He had almost decided to turn away when he recognized that two of the aircraft were Spads. When he drew closer, he could see that they were attempting to attack a German two seater that was trying to make it back across the lines.

The pilot of the two seater was clever and the observer must have been a good shot. Whenever one of the Spads dove to the attack, the pilot always managed to turn so that the Spad had no shot, but his gunner, shooting to the rear, had a clear one. The Spads were not aggressive, but seemed to be content to keep the two seater from returning to his own lines.

Luke saw that if he could gain another two hundred feet he could use the cloud ahead of him as cover and probably pass very close to the two seater. Occupied with the Spads behind him, the German pilot seemed not to have noticed Luke's Spad up against the base of the clouds.

Luke pushed the power up to 1800 RPMs. The engine shook as if it would tear itself to pieces, but the Spad climbed and soon Luke had a cloud between himself and the other three aircraft. He checked his guns. There were only a dozen or so rounds left for the Vickers and perhaps twenty for the 45. It would be enough. One chance was the best he could hope for.

He came clear of the cloud and saw the German two seater closing rapidly from off to his right. Both the pilot and the observer were watching the Spads to their rear. The two seater passed no more than a hundred feet in front of him and Luke stitched a line of bullet holes all down the length of the fuselage.

The engine stopped and the pilot and gunner both slumped over in their cockpits. The two seater fell off on the right wing and began a slow spiral down behind the allied lines. There was no fire or smoke.

The engine in Luke's Spad quit again. Again there was no pressure in the main tank. He switched to the gravity fed emergency tank in the upper wing. The engine quickly caught, but even with the power pulled back to 1400 RPMs it shook violently. The water temperature was also beginning to rise. He needed to get on the ground.

He descended to the west, looking for a smooth field large enough to allow him to make a landing. The ground behind the lines had been heavily fought over in the past and was marked with shell holes and crossed with trenches. The roads were muddy and the ruts were filled with water. What he wanted was a pasture with some grass on it.

What he got was a narrow plowed field alongside an artillery battery. It had two advantages. The first was that it was dead into the wind. The second was that if he flipped the Spad over, the artillery crews would come running and get him out.

He came across the artillery battery at some five hundred feet and turned to align himself with the plowed field next to it. When he was sure that he had the field made, he closed the throttle, shut off the fuel and cut both magnetos.

The muddy furrows came up slowly to meet him and he held the Spad off until it would fly no more. The touch down was easy, but the Spad immediately dropped the right wing and turned sharply to the right. It slid for a second, almost sideways, until the left wing came down and dug into the mud and then it spun 180 degrees to the left and came to a stop tipped at a funny angle.

Luke pulled himself out of the cockpit and jumped down into the mud. The Spad was a wreck. It would never fly again. He walked around it marveling at how much damage it had taken and still not come apart in the air. There were more than a dozen bullet holes just from the cockpit back to the tail. The right wheel was gone. Whether it had been shot off in the air or broken off in the landing, he could not tell. The wings were almost sieved with holes and there was a large chunk torn out of the leading edge of the upper right wing. He passed around to the front and saw that a bullet had struck one blade of the propeller and broken off half of it. The was the reason that the engine had vibrated so badly. The main spars of both lower wings had been broken in the landing. There was no telling what other unseen damage there was. But it had brought him home.

Behind him he heard cheering and yelling and he turned around to see more than a dozen of the gun crew running toward him through the muddy field. He stepped out clear of the plane so that they could see that he was all right. Still they came running on as hard as they could go. When they were closer, he could see that the uniforms were French.

They reached him almost all together and they milled around for a moment, all shouting at once in French, and then the two largest picked him up and set him up on their shoulders. It was only then that they seemed to realize that he was an American.

The one officer quieted them and spoke to Luke in fairly good English. They had seen the two balloons burn on the horizon and the two seater had crashed not a quarter of a mile to the south of them. But there was more. They were linked by field phone to a French observation balloon and the observer had given them a running account of the entire fight.

He had seen a Spad burn first one balloon and then the other. At that time, two Fokkers had come down from above the clouds and another Spad had shot one down and was firing on the second when they had disappeared from sight below the trees. Four other Fokkers had come down in pursuit of that Spad and then two more had attacked the Spad that had burned the balloon. These he had turned on and shot down, 'Bang, bang.' Then Luke had come out of nowhere and shot down the two seater that the two French Spads had been unable to get. Was he by any chance the pilot that had shot down the balloons?

Luke told them that he was. "Cinque, cinque," the officer told the men and they all cheered. For the first time it registered on Luke that he had gained five victories in little more than ten minutes. They started to carry him off toward the guns when he remembered his automatic. One of the men got it for him out of the cockpit.

They carried him, on their shoulders, almost a hundred yards to where the command post for the battery was located. The men in the battery, when they heard that he was the pilot that had burned the two balloons and shot down the two Fokkers in addition to the two seater, waved their caps and cheered. Confirmation had already been received on all five and on the Fokker shot down by Wehner, as well.

There was a motorcycle in the battery and Luke got one of the men to take him on it to their company headquarters where there was a telephone. As before, they were not able to connect him to the American system so that he could talk to Rembercourt, but they did connect him with the duty officer at the Storks. He got someone who could speak English and Luke gave him the information on his victories and Wehner's that he wanted passed on to Rembercourt and to Major Hartney at Group Headquarters.

Rene Foucet came on the phone then at the Storks and insisted that Luke tell him what had happened in detail. Every so often, he would have Luke stop and Luke would hear him telling the story in French. The pilots of the two French Spads that had been attacking the two seater had landed only minutes before and had told, in wonderment, how an American Spad had appeared out of thin air and knocked the two seater down with a full 90 degree deflection shot. When Rene explained that it was Luke's fifth victory that afternoon, everyone in the operations rooms must have tried to talk at once for Luke heard a dozen or more voices cry out in amazement.

Luke asked if Wehner had by any chance landed at the Storks. Rene said he had not and asked in return how long they had been up. Luke looked at his watch and saw that little more than an hour had passed since he and Wehner had taken off. Rene would ask about Wehner when he called Rembercourt and Group Headquarters. A car was already on the way to pick up Luke. Rene expected that they would know something by the time Luke arrived at the Storks.

They were sending a photographer with the driver. The two

seater was the first of Luke's victories to fall on the allied side of the lines and they wanted to be sure and get a picture of him standing in front of the wreckage. The party would start as soon as Luke returned with the crosses cut out of the fabric of the two seater's wings.

Chapter 13

☆ ☆ ☆

It was the morning of September 20th. Gathered in the mess of the 27th Squadron were some two dozen journalists representing newspapers in every country on the allied side. The story of Luke's amazing five victories in ten minutes had spread quickly throughout all the armies and made him the most talked about soldier on either side of the line. Now, every reporter in France that could secure authorization, had gathered at Rembercourt to pay homage to America's new Ace of Aces and to hear his story first hand.

They were to have some time to wait. Coffee and biscuits and jam had been put out and most of the men had helped themselves. Many had come away without their breakfasts in order to catch the official cars that the air service had provided. Only one of them, Jay Harrison from the New York Times, had ever met Luke. A group had gathered around him to glean whatever information he was willing to share.

Major Hartney and Captain Grant came in and there was a little stir as the correspondents found their chairs and settled down. "Which one is Luke?" someone asked.

Hartney took the podium that had been set up at the end of the room. "I am Major Hartney, Commander of the 1st Pursuit Group," he said abruptly. "This is Captain Grant, Commander of the 27th Pursuit Squadron."

"All of you know by now that Lieutenant Frank Luke destroyed two balloons and three enemy aircraft the day before yesterday. "Many of you have questions. Before I take them, I'd like to tell you exactly what happened and, hopefully, clear up the misunderstandings that some of you seem to have."

The was a restless stirring among the correspondents. They wanted to see Luke. He was the news. Hartney ignored them and went on. "The day before yesterday, at about three in the afternoon, an order came down asking us to destroy two balloons that had recently been put up at Labeauville. We expected them to be heavily defended both by guns on the ground and Fokkers in the air."

"We sent a total of sixteen aircraft against them. Fourteen, that were designated as high cover, were led by Captain Grant here. Luke and Lieutenant Joe Wehner were to attack the balloons and they made their approach separately, just at the base of the clouds."

"In less than ten minutes from the time he began his attack on the first balloon, Luke burned two balloons, shot down two Fokkers behind the German lines and then a two seat observation plane just inside the allied lines. As far as I know, he is the first pilot to achieve that many confirmed victories in a single mission. Wehner also had a Fokker confirmed as did Captain Vasconcelles, our operations officer, and Captain Rickenbacker, the commander of the 94th Pursuit Group."

"Where's Luke," one of the reporters asked?"

"We were told that we were coming out here to meet him," another demanded.

"All in good time," Hartney answered, obviously irritated. "But first I ought to explain something to you about military courtesy. I am the ranking officer here and I am conducting this briefing. If you will give me your undivided attention, by the time that I have finished, some of you will have gained enough understanding of what took place to ask intelligent questions. Those of you who are too impatient to do that are free to leave at this time."

There was dead silence and no one moved. Hartney went on. "Luke's Spad was so badly damaged by enemy fire that he had to land at a French artillery battery not far from the field where the Storks are based. They sent a car for him and he spent the night there. Luke has a lot of friends over there among the French pilots and I understand they threw him quite a party. He returned here yesterday and last night Colonel Mitchell came down from headquarters and Captain Rickenbacker and some of the others came over from the 94th and we gave a party for Luke ourselves."

"I need to tell you," Hartney said solemnly, "That, although a celebration was clearly in order, none of our hearts were really in it. You see, we sent out sixteen aircraft and only got fifteen back.

Considering that we destroyed six enemy aircraft and two balloons at a cost of only one of our own aircraft, we had, at least on paper, a very productive day. In my estimation, it was a disastrous day; for Joe Wehner, the pilot of the missing plane, was worth far more than any six aircraft or any two balloons."

"Lieutenant Wehner, who has flown with Luke on every patrol this past week and who had just scored his eighth victory, was last seen firing on a Fokker that was diving low over the German lines. Several other Fokkers were diving on Wehner from behind. When Wehner did not return, we hoped to hear that he had made an emergency landing somewhere behind our lines. When it became obvious that that had not happened, we hoped that he had landed successfully behind the enemy lines and was a prisoner or in a hospital there. Beyond that, there was always the chance that he had somehow managed to elude the Germans and was hiding in a barn or a woods somewhere on the other side of the lines."

"Early this morning, a report from the International Red Cross put an end to all those hopes. Joe Wehner was killed instantly when his Spad crashed behind enemy lines the afternoon of September 18th."

Hartney stopped to blow his nose and wipe his eyes. "It was something we all expected, but didn't want to admit. Luke particularly, insisted that Wehner would come walking up to the mess some morning, asking if breakfast was ready, but like the rest of us, he must have guessed the worst."

Captain Holden, the surgeon, came in then and took Hartney off to the side and spoke to him in private. Holden went out and Hartney again took the podium. "It may be some time before you are able to see Lieutenant Luke. The last two days have been especially difficult for him. On the one hand, there was the excitement of all those victories one right after the other and then the waiting for Wehner to call in and the hours of hoping that somehow he would turn up alive. You see, Luke hasn't been here long enough to learn that the first rule of war is, 'don't make friends.' Luke and Wehner were best friends. They roomed together. They flew every mission together. Together, they were the deadliest pair that I have ever seen."

"Luke was in such a state last night that the surgeon finally had to give him an injection to get him to sleep. He's still sleeping. When he wakes up we are going to have to give him the official report on Wehner and then it will take him some time to get cleaned up and ready to talk to you. I hope that all of you can somehow understand the sense of loss that he is sure to feel. For Luke, the fact that Wehner is dead will make all of his victories meaningless. You won't see him cry though. He's too tough for that." Hartney stopped to again blow his nose and wipe his eyes. "That's only for old fools like me who have spent years at the front and still haven't learned not to make friends."

There was a long, awkward silence then while Hartney struggled to regain his composure." I know you have all come here to see Luke," Hartney went on finally. "But first I want to say a few words about Lieutenant Wehner. Most of you are probably unaware of the fact, but he was in Hamburg with his father in 1916, and worked for a time there as an orderly, tending wounded German soldiers in a military hospital. America was neutral at the time and his actions were perfectly proper, but that kind of thing was looked at with suspicion by any number of people. Many questioned his patriotism. Many questioned his motives for volunteering for the Air Service. He was even investigated by the Secret Service."

There was a buzz among the correspondents at that piece of news. "I never doubted him for a moment," Hartney continued. "He was a natural pilot from the first day he went up and he was as fine an officer as I have ever had the opportunity to command. It was already arranged that at the end of the war, because of his fluency in German, he was to be transferred to General Pershing's staff where he was to assist in the occupation and disarmament of Germany. I expected that one day he would take his place on the world stage as a statesman or an international financier. It goes down hard, to lose a man like that."

The correspondents were strangely quiet. They had come to cheer a hero, but Hartney's manner and his remarks had quieted them.

"Perhaps I've said enough," Hartney said abruptly. "Perhaps now would be the time for me to take some of your questions."

A few minutes before there had been a hundred questions, but Hartney's sobering introduction had taken the correspondents a little by surprise and they now hung back. Finally, one of the British correspondents asked, "If my information is correct, ten days ago Lieutenant Luke didn't have a single victory and now with thirteen, he's the leading American ace. To what do you attribute this sudden success?"

"Well," Hartney hesitated. "Opportunity, mostly. Luke's always had the ability, but since Chateau Thierry the Germans have been avoiding combat and it's pretty hard to get a victory when you can't get a fight. In this latest offensive we've been asked to take down a few balloons and they, of course, can't run away. Beyond that, the Germans have put up some Fokkers to try and protect their balloons."

"Any particular reason for Luke's great success against balloons?"

Hartney hesitated again. "He isn't afraid," he said finally. "And he's a dead shot, by far the best shot that any of us have ever seen or heard of."

"What difference would that make against something as big as a balloon?"

"Well, you have to understand the mechanics of the thing," Hartney said. "The balloon is full of hydrogen, but hydrogen by itself won't burn or support combustion. You can fire a red hot bullet into one side of a balloon and it will come out the other side cool enough to hold in your hand. In order to get a balloon to burn you have to punch or tear a good sized piece out of the top of it and then, when the hydrogen and the oxygen in the air have had a chance to mix, then, and only then, an incendiary bullet has a chance of setting it off. It takes a marksman like Luke to consistently put a couple dozen rounds into a spot the size of a dinner plate and burn a balloon on the first pass."

"Most of Luke's victories are over balloons. Isn't that somewhat unusual.?" The question came from another British correspondent.

"Not really," Hartney answered. "Every balloon he's done has been a command performance in support of the offensive against St. Mihiel. The only Fokkers that he and Whener have had time for are the ones that have gotten in their way. And both Luke and Whener have had victories over Fokkers this week that we haven't been able to be confirm because they were shot down so far behind the German lines."

"If Whener was such an outstanding pilot," One of the American correspondents asked, "How do you explain his death?"

Hartney waited for a moment to reply. He was obviously irritated by the question. How was it, he thought, that anyone was killed. It was a war. Soldiers were shooting at one another with real bullets. Every now and then someone got hit. Talent didn't always have a lot to do with it. In 1915, two weeks after he had been posted to flight training, his entire platoon of 48 men had been killed when the Germans had set off a mine beneath their front line trench.

He calmed himself and gave the man an answer. "The Vickers, 30 caliber guns fire at a rate of 400 rounds per minute, that's almost 7 shots per second. The German Spandau guns fire at about the same rate. With two guns firing, a three second burst puts out some forty shots. In any engagement of several aircraft all swirling around one another, there can be a lot of lead flying through the air at any one time. It only takes one lucky shot that hits the pilot or some vital part of the aircraft to bring it down."

"Look at Von Richthofen," Hartney went on. "Once he became famous, he seldom flew without a half dozen Aces at his back. I never thought that anyone would get him. And yet, Captain Brown did, with a single bullet through the heart. Wehner and Luke weren't anywhere near as cautious as Richthofen, you'll see that when we have a look at some of the airplanes that they managed to bring back. When he was last seen, Wehner had just shot down one Fokker and was in the process of shooting down another. Still, there were four or five more Fokkers behind him. If one British Camel could bring down the great Richthofen, I guess it would not be unreasonable for four or five Fokkers to bring down Wehner."

"How would you compare Luke to Richthofen," someone asked.

"Compare Luke to Richthofen," Hartney mused. "Well, Richthofen with eighty confirmed victories is the most famous pilot to have ever flown on this or any other front. He was in active combat for almost three years, he originated many of what are now standard tactics, he formed the famous Flying Circus. Some of you may know that I have some personal knowledge of the man. He was supposed to be my 6th victory; instead, I became his 28th. I was lucky enough to crash in no-man's-land and do no more than break both ankles. A couple of Tommies crawled out and dragged me in to their trenches just minutes before the German artillery dropped a shell right on my plane."

"Then you wouldn't put Luke in Richthofen's league?"

"Not as a leader, not as a Squadron Commander, not necessarily as an innovator, although Luke probably knows as much about burning balloons as anyone, with the possible exception of the Belgian, Coppens. The thing about Luke that you have to keep in mind," Hartney said, "Is that he has run up 13 victories in a week; 5 of them in one combat patrol. Richthofen never had a day or a week to compare to that. He was cautious and let his men take all the chances, and he never attacked unless he was at a clear advantage. On average, he had fewer than three victories a month."

"So in a fight between the two, who would come out on top?"

"You mean as a staged match, with no other aircraft involved?" Hartney said.

"Yes."

"If they could meet now," Hartney said. "In equal aircraft with neither having the advantage of altitude or position, Luke would kill Richthofen within the first minute."

There was a period of silence while the correspondents scribbled that remark into their notes. It was the kind of definitive quote that their editors wanted to read.

"On what do you base that opinion?" one finally asked.

Hartney started to reply and then caught himself and took a different tack. "Most pilots take a lot of pride in their airplanes; they paint slogans or emblems on them or name them after their wives or girl friends. Some of the Spads in Rickenbacker's squadron are painted up as gaudy as circus wagons. Nungesser's Spad has a skull and crossbones in a big red heart on the side of the fuselage. And most of you know that Richtoffen had his triplane painted a blood red so that when you saw him behind you, you knew that your number was up."

"Luke's not like that. To him a Spad is only a machine that can carry him and two machine guns up to where he can do some damage. His airplane is as expendable as an Apache's horse. He goes where he wants to go and forces the airplane to go with him, the consequences be damned. He attacks with such a fury and turns so quickly and is such a dead shot that I don't see how anyone could stand up to him in a single combat."

There was again a period of silence while the correspondents got that information into their notes.

"Would the Spad and the Fokker be considered equal aircraft?" The question came from a French correspondent.

"Well," Hartney thought a minute. "Equal perhaps, but not similar. The Spad is a much bigger, heavier machine and it will out dive the Fokker. The Fokker is smaller and lighter and will out climb the Spad and probably out turn it."

"We've heard it said that this new Fokker is the best pursuit of the war?"

Hartney thought about that for a minute. "It's certainly the best

German pursuit. Whether it can out fly the Camel or the Spad is something we probably won't know for sure until after the war when we can really test one against the other."

"Do you like the Spad better than the Camel?" It was the British correspondent again.

"The Camel is probably my choice," Hartney said. "Originally we were supposed to fly them. Matter of fact, I had a victory in one this summer. But the Spad is all right. The Hispano-Suiza engine is a very reliable, all aluminum V-8 with a lot of power. And you can point a Spad straight at the ground with full power on and let it run up to its maximum speed and not worry about tearing the wings off either in the dive or the pull out."

"Is it true," One of the American correspondents asked. "That Luke did so poorly at Issoudun that he had to repeat a portion of his advanced training?"

"That is true," Hartney said. "But not unusual. Many pilots are required to repeat a portion of their training. Combat flying leaves little room for mistakes. The Spad, like any high performance machine, requires constant attention to the engine and flight instruments. In addition, the pilot has to keep his place in the formation, keep his eye on his flight leader and also keep a sharp lookout for enemy aircraft. In a fight, it gets even more complicated. The neat formation breaks up, guns jam, engines overheat, perhaps the flight leader goes down, but still, every pilot must keep a cool head and get himself home. Even the best trained pilots have difficulty in their first few patrols. To send a man out that wasn't ready would be cold blooded murder."

"Did you think that Luke was ready when he was assigned to you?"

"Oh yes," Hartney said. "Because Luke graduated in the bottom half of his class, he was first assigned to ferry new Spads from the factory to the front and he spent over a month doing that. Whatever deficiencies he might have had, he corrected them during that time. Most replacement pilots that we get require a series of training and familiarization flights before they are ready to do combat patrols. Luke was ready for combat the day he arrived. He was, by far, the best replacement we have ever received."

"What conclusions do you draw from that?"

Hartney thought for a moment. "It would be easy to say that new pilots should have more flying time before they are sent into combat. With a war going on though, an extended training period is an expensive luxury. Eventually, every man has to fly his first combat patrol and, on that patrol and the next four or five after it, he has to learn more than he did in his three months at Issoudun. The Germans give the final examinations and they are hard markers. They never take into account a man's previous record."

"But you said before, that when Luke came to the squadron he had nothing to learn?"

"No," Hartney answered. "I said he was the best prepared replacement that we had ever received. The time never comes when a pilot has nothing left to learn. Since he has been here, Luke has learned enough to begin giving lessons to all the rest of us. His ability to learn is one of the reasons he has been so successful."

"Could you give us an example of that?"

"I could give you several," Hartney said. "But I'll have to decline on the basis of military security. Burning balloons is dangerous enough as it is without us giving away any secrets."

"Just how dangerous is it?"

"How dangerous," Hartney said. "If you'd like, we'll walk outside now and you can take a look at some of the aircraft that Luke and Wehner managed to bring back this week and you can judge for yourselves how dangerous it is."

The correspondents followed Hartney out on to the field and over behind one of the hangers where a dozen Spads in various stages of decay were parked. Hartney stopped at the second in line. The propeller and the wheels had been removed and there was a dark smear of oil underneath the engine. The wings and the fuselage were riddled with holes. "This was Luke's first plane," Hartney said. "He shot down his first balloon in it on the morning of the 12th, the opening day of the battle for St. Mihiel."

The correspondents crowded around the plane. Some began to count the bullet holes.

"Don't waste your time counting the holes," Hartney said. "They've been counted before and the number never comes out the same. Four hundred is probably pretty close to the fact."

"How could they hit him so many times and not bring him down?"

"Well," Hartney answered. "They didn't hit Luke, which is about the only thing they missed. If you'll look, you'll see that the fuselage and wings are mostly fabric and air. A hole or two in the fabric doesn't mean much. The engine and the pilot and the gas tank are what count. In this case, when Luke landed at one of our observation posts just this side of the line, the engine was running on no more than four cylinders and was in the process of beating itself to pieces."

They moved over one airplane. "This," Hartney said. "Was the plane that Luke flew when he got his second balloon on the 14th. The radiator was shot full of holes and with the coolant gone, the engine froze. Beside that, the lower main spar is damaged so that the airframe can't be easily repaired."

The next aircraft was missing both the propeller and the complete engine and radiator assembly. It did not seem as badly damaged as the first two although there was a dark stain around and below the cockpit. "Luke got his third balloon in this plane," Hartney said. "It burned on the first pass, but a Fokker hit him as he pulled away and punctured the main fuel tank under the seat. Why it didn't burn, I don't know. Wehner shot two Fokkers off of Luke's tail to allow him to get home. When Luke landed his flying suit was soaked with gasoline. His goggles saved his eyes."

"What happened to the engine?" Someone asked.

"Oh, it was fine," Hartney said. "But Luke asked to never fly this airplane again. You can imagine how he felt the whole time he was bringing it back when the slightest spark would have set him afire. If he didn't want to fly it again, I didn't think anyone else should have to. The engine had only a few hours time on it, so we were able to install it on another plane."

They passed two other wrecks that were not Luke's and then they came to a pair of Spads parked together a little way from the others. Close inspection revealed that they were riddled with holes and that some of the fabric was missing.

"These are the Spads that Luke and Wehner flew the night they burned three balloons in less than a minute's time," Hartney said. "One or even both may be repairable. We just haven't had the time to do a thorough inspection for structural damage."

Finally they came to the most pathetic wreck of all. One wheel was missing, both lower main spars were broken and the wings tilted up at an awkward angle. Mud was spattered all over the lower half of the aircraft. Bullet holes were everywhere and a large piece of fabric was missing from the leading edge and the upper surface of the top right wing. Half of one propeller blade had been shot away.

"This is the plane that Luke flew on his last patrol when he bagged the two balloons, the two Fokkers and the Halberstat,"

Hartney said.

The correspondents walked around the wreckage, looking at the bullet holes and trying to imagine what could drive a man to continue on the attack with so crippled a machine. One of them stopped to write a comment in his note pad. A second, looking over his shoulder, read, 'Death rarely withholds his hand when persistently and continuously flaunted.'

"Amen," the second correspondent said.

"Is this usual?" another of the correspondents asked. "To bring back an aircraft so badly damaged from almost every patrol?"

"Hardly," Hartney answered. "I've never heard of anyone bringing back four nonrepairables in a single week. On the other hand, no one has ever downed ten balloons and three aircraft in a single week."

"What about Rickenbacker?" one of the Americans asked. "Does he bring home aircraft shot up as badly as these?"

Hartney thought for a moment. "Sometime around the Fourth of July, Rickenbacker got one of the first three new Spads assigned to the 94th. Since that time, he has had four or five confirmed victories. And he is still flying his original Spad."

"To what do you attribute that?"

"Oh, well, luck to some extent," Hartney said. "Rick comes home with a few holes now and then, but nothing that can't be fixed with a patch and some glue. He is cautious and only attacks when he sees a situation that he can exploit. And, all his victories have been over enemy aircraft. Attacking balloons at low altitude with dozens of guns shooting at you from the ground and Fokkers waiting overhead to jump you when you come off the target is all together another thing."

A corporal came down from the operations room then and announced that Luke was in the officer's mess and ready to meet with the correspondents. They fell in behind Hartney and made their way back along the line of broken Spads.

In the mess, the Frank Luke that they saw was not the 'Laughing eyed terror of the German Balloon Corps.' that the correspondent from the New York Times had seen the night he had visited the 27th with Colonel Mitchell. Luke's eyes were hard and his jaw was grimly set. His answers to the correspondents questions, though polite, were short. He volunteered no information on his own. Forewarned by Hartney, no one asked about Joe Wehner and the interview soon came to an end.

Some of the correspondents had brought photographers with them and Luke consented to having his picture taken standing next to a new Spad. Arms folded across his chest, one foot set casually in front of the other as he leaned ever so easily against the forward edge of the lower wing. Luke, with his fresh young face and his blonde hair brushed back hardly looked like America's Ace of Aces. It was his eyes that gave him away. Steely blue eyes that looked not at the camera or at the correspondents, but focused rather on the far eastern horizon where there just might be another German sausage, swaying gently in the wind.

The photographers did their work and when they were finished Luke went back to his quarters. The correspondents, in small groups, made their way back to the mess where their cars were waiting. "Did you see those eyes?" one said to another. "How would you like to look over your shoulder and see those eyes staring at you through a gun sight?"

"Did you see those planes all shot up?" another said. "Jesus Christ, once would be bad enough. But can you see him going back day after day? How the hell does he do it?"

Hartney was walking along with the correspondents and heard the remark. "You might more correctly ask, how any of us does it." he told them. "Being a pursuit pilot in this war is a mighty dangerous trade when you work at it every day. You've only seen the damaged airplanes that the pilots managed to nurse back across the lines. For every one of those there are at least two more out there somewhere that crashed and burned and those represent the loss not only of an airplane, but the pilot as well."

"So how do all of you do it?"

Hartney had stopped and a group of the correspondents had gathered around him. "How do we do it? A patrol at a time, I guess. Why do we do it? I suppose everyone has their own reasons. For a lot of men whose fathers were foreign born, patriotism certainly has something to do with it. After what has happened this past week, it's certain that no one will ever question Luke or Whener or Rickenbacker's loyalty based on the fact that their fathers came from Germany."

"Again, in Luke's case," Hartney told them, "pride has a lot to do with it. Ever since he was assigned to us, Luke has had what most of the pilots in the squadron considered an exaggerated sense of his own ability. As it turns out, he knew exactly what he was talking about and this past week has given him a chance to prove it. No matter how heavy the ground fire was or how many Fokkers were up or how badly his plane was damaged, Luke never failed to bring down every balloon that we sent him after. That kind of tenacity and determination indicate to me that in pilots like Luke, and Wehner, we are seeing an entirely different breed of cat. We probably need to do more to identify them early in their training and see that they get assigned to pursuit squadrons where they will have a chance to show what they can do."

"So what happens to Luke now?"

"Leave," Hartney said. "That boy has compressed what would be a magnificent year for any combat pilot into a single week. And he's seen his best friend killed, protecting him. He may not realize it, but he needs to get away from all of this for a time. He's going to Paris for a week and take in the sights. After he gets back, we'll see if we can't work out a way for him to get his victories without taking so much fire in return."

Chapter 14

It was the 27th of September, just six days after Luke had been sent to Paris with Captain Holden, the Squadron Surgeon. Holden stood in Hartney's office at Group Headquarters, waiting for him to finish a phone call.

"Did you get my message?" Holden asked as soon as Hartney had put the phone down.

Hartney nodded.

"I don't know where he went," Holden went on. "When I found out that Luke had checked out of the hotel, I didn't know what to do except to send you a message and come on back."

"Sit down," Hartney said as he slid a piece of paper across his desk. "Take a look at this."

Captain Holden sat down and scanned the sheet. "Fokker confirmed Sept. 26, 16:30 hours. Claimed by Lt. Frank Luke," he read in amazement. "But how could this be?"

"You know that he hooked up with Nungesser and a couple of the other Storks in Paris?"

"Yes," Holden said. "They came by the hotel for him the first morning. I wondered how they knew that we were there?"

"I arranged it," Hartney said. "But go on."

"Well, they asked me to come along, but I didn't want to throw a wet blanket on anything they might have had in mind, so I declined. They usually came in when the sun was coming up and one night they didn't even come in at all, but I saw Luke almost every day. If we didn't have lunch together, he always left me a message. Then yesterday, when I asked at the desk for my messages, they told me that he had checked out."

"Yes," Hartney said. "I've just finished talking to Nungesser. It seems that they had just about had their fill of Paris night life and they were thinking about doing a little flying, to sort of clear their heads, you know. When Nungesser called Orley to see if there were any planes that they could fly, he found out that they had four new Spads with high performance engines that they wanted flown to the Storks. Nungesser called a taxi and they left for the airport immediately."

"When they got to the Storks," Hartney went on. "They were so impressed with the way the new Spads flew with the bigger engines that they decided to fly a combat patrol. They had the planes refueled and the guns armed and off they went, southeast, down the front line. Not thirty minutes later, they spotted four, red nosed Fokkers coming the opposite way, just over the German trenches. They went for the Fokkers and the Fokkers went for them."

"Nungesser said that it was the greatest fight that he had ever experienced. The confident way that the Fokkers came at them made Nungesser sure that the leader was Udet himself. Once engaged, he was certain that every one of the Germans was an Ace, as were the French pilots and Luke. The eight of them, with certainly over a hundred victories between them, began what he called the 'Danse Macabre.'"

"They changed partners at every turn, knowing that the first one to miss a step was a dead man. Sometimes they passed within feet of each other, but the pattern that they flew was so tight that no one could bring his guns to bear. Observers said that the fight lasted less than three or four minutes. Nungesser said that he lost all track of time, that he thought that they must have dueled for half an hour."

"Finally, Luke got the slightest crack of an opening and killed one of the German pilots with a short burst, only a half dozen rounds from each gun, Nungesser said. The Fokker fell almost directly into the front line of the German trenches. The others immediately broke off the fight and dove directly into their own lines where they had the protection of all the guns on the ground."

"The Germans didn't stay to try and avenge their fallen comrade?" Captain Holden interrupted.

"No," Hartney answered. "In that kind of company it would have been a mistake. Like playing hockey with a man in the penalty box, one opponent would have always been uncovered. Udet did the right thing when he cut and ran."

"Luke didn't get Udet then?" Holden said.

"Not this time," Hartney said. "Udet flies with a red and white streamer tied to the tail skid so that the rest of the flight can spot him. One of the Fokkers that escaped had a red and white streamer attached to the skid."

"Does Grant know about this?"

"Oh yes," Hartney said. "He knew before I did. He called me over an hour ago."

"What did he think about it all?"

"You can well imagine," Hartney rolled his eyes in his head. "As soon as he found out about it, he called the Storks and insisted on speaking to Luke. He demanded an explanation and Luke said that he was still on leave, that he could do as he pleased."

Holden laughed.

"Grant didn't think that it was so funny," Hartney said. "He ordered Luke to report back to Rembercourt today. Luke said that if Grant wanted him back so bad, he'd have to send a car for him as the Storks had none to spare."

Holden laughed again. "It gets better all the time."

"Not for me it doesn't," Hartney said. "Grant intends to court martial Luke unless Luke makes a complete and public apology for all of the stunts he's pulled."

"Grant told you this?"

"No, the Sergeant Major showed me the preliminary document when I was there a few days ago. He thought I ought to know what was in the works."

"What would his charges be?" Holden asked.

"Insubordination, striking a fellow officer, leaving a formation without permission, threatening an officer of a friendly government with a hand grenade and now, flying combat with a foreign power without authorization."

"He'd have a hard time getting a guilty verdict," Holden said.

"That could be. But how am I going to explain to Mitchell and Pershing and the American press that our Ace of Aces is being court-martialed."

"You need to get him out of the 27th," Holden said. "Transfer him over to Rickenbacker at the 94th, or anywhere."

"That's what Nungesser said when I talked to him just now. He suggested that we discharge Luke and let him enlist in the Foreign Legion, assigned to the Storks. Can you imagine explaining that to the American press?"

"Give him to Rick then, if he'll have him."

"Oh he'd have him in a minute. I've talked to him about it more than once. He could handle Luke because Luke respects him. Rick would have taken both Luke and Wehner, but that was the problem. Grant would have been glad to see Luke go, but Wehner was an officer that no commander would surrender without a fight. And once they started flying together, there was no way that I could separate Luke and Wehner. Now Grant won't let Luke go because he wants him out of the Air Service all together. Grant, on top of everything else, thinks that Luke is insane."

"Insane?"

Hartney nodded. "That's why I sent you with Luke. I wanted you to spend some time with him and then ask your opinion."

Holden shook his head. "If Luke is insane, then God help the rest of us. I never saw anyone as solid or as sane in my life. The fact that he's done some crazy stuff only proves my point. In a week's time he's become the best known soldier in the allied armies and he's lost his best friend. I think, for a boy that by all rights should be on a college campus somewhere with a pretty girl on his arm, he's handled himself pretty well."

"Tell me about your trip," Hartney said.

"Well, we started out about like you'd expect. Luke was a little sullen about being ordered on leave and you could see that he was still brooding about Wehner's death. Then, not long after we'd started, a Captain and a Lieutenant came through our car and the Captain recognized Luke from a picture that had been in the paper. He introduced himself and shook Luke's hand and then he sat down opposite us and told one of the damnedest stories I have ever heard."

"The Captain commanded a Company in the Iowa Regiment of the Rainbow Division. They were in the first line of troops to attack at Chateau Thierry and they went over in the fog with only fifty yards visibility. They stumbled right into a line of German machine gun nests and had no chance at all. In the first twenty minutes, they took sixty percent casualties. By the end of the day, they had so many dead and wounded that had to be taken out of the line."

"Again, at St. Mihiel, the Company was in the front line. Again the visibility was low because of fog and rain. The men that had been at Chateau Thierry were not anxious to repeat that experience again and the replacements were not battle hardened troops.

At the first sign of resistance, they went to ground and even when the enemy artillery began to range on them, they wouldn't move except at a crawl."

"The Captain was frantic. He knew if they stayed where they were the German artillery would chop them up and they would also lose the advantage of advancing behind the moving barrage that the American artillery was laying down. But nothing would get the men to move."

"And then, directly in front of them, they saw this kind of glow above the fog. In a minute, it was brighter and they could tell that it was something very large that was burning. He said it looked like someone had lit a giant bonfire in the sky. For the first time that morning, the men's' spirits lifted."

"He passed the word that the fire was their objective. That they would camp there for the night and cook their suppers over the hot ashes. Men that only minutes before wouldn't get off their bellies, stood up and began to advance. The enemy resistance was nothing compared to what they had experienced at Chateau Thierry and they carried the first German trench right on schedule. By three o'clock in the afternoon, they had advanced so far that they were ordered to halt and wait for the flanks to come up."

"A day or two later the Captain found out that it was Luke who had burned the balloon. And when he saw Frank there in the train, there just wasn't anything he wouldn't have done for him. He insisted that we move up to the next car with him where there were a bunch of officers from the Rainbow Division going on leave."

"They were all laughing and having a good time and on the floor they had going a crap game to end all crap games. Everyone had to be introduced to Frank. All of them had seen him burn at least one balloon and they didn't hesitate to tell him what life was like with a big German sausage hanging on the horizon so that they couldn't even show themselves to go and take a crap."

"Before long, they had Frank down there on the floor with them and in the hour that it took us to get into Paris he had the damnedest run of luck with the dice that I have ever seen. When we pulled into the station he had wads of dollars and francs stuffed into every pocket. He had to have won close to five hundred dollars and there wasn't a man in the car that begrudged him a dime of it. The Germans don't have a lot of shells to waste and they won't fire unless they have a definite target. Whenever Frank brought down a balloon, he silenced all the German artillery in that part of the line."

"I didn't know that Frank was a gambler," Hartney interjected.

"There are a lot of things that we didn't know about him," Holden said. "And it gets more interesting as you go along. When we got a cab at the station, he insisted on going to Notre Dame, even before we checked into the hotel. When we got there he had me find him an English speaking priest to hear his confession. My French isn't that good, but I managed and pretty soon this older priest came out and he and Frank went into one of the confessionals along the wall. I can't imagine what he would have had to confess. Hell, we had only arrived in Paris, but they were there for some time. After that he went to take communion and he had the priest ask all those who were in the church to take communion with him if they wanted. A couple of dozen or so came forward. They knew by his uniform that he was an American flyer, but whether they recognized him as Frank Luke or not, I don't know. After he had received communion, Frank started bringing all his gambling money out of his pockets and counting it out into the priest's hand."

"Buying masses for Joe Wehner?" Hartney asked.

"That and candles," Holden answered. "They had the altar boys bringing them out by the armloads. There must have been several hundred all blazing at once at one of the side alters. A half dozen more priests came out to meet Frank and quite a stir began to go through the church. Not wanting to start any kind of commotion, Frank had them let us out through a side door and we came on to the hotel."

"We got our rooms and Frank said that what he wanted most was to get a hot bath and soak for awhile. I got a bath and a change of clothes and about six I went down to Frank's room to see what he wanted to do about dinner. He was still in a bath robe and said that he was too tired to go out, that he would have them send up a sandwich or something and that he would turn in early. He did look tired, so I said that I would meet him for breakfast at eight and left him to himself."

"I went down and sat in the lobby, thinking that someone I knew might come by and have dinner with me. There was a surgeon there from the First Division and we got to talking. He was waiting for a friend of his that was assigned to a convalescent hospital there in Paris. When his friend showed up, they asked me to have dinner with them. When I told them who had come up to Paris with me they were really impressed. The one especially, since he

A BONFIRE IN THE SKY

had lived in Arizona and knew Frank's father and some of his brothers and sisters."

"That right?" Hartney said. "What did he have to say about Frank?"

"Oh, plenty," Holden said. "Our boy had some kind of reputation before he ever got into the Air Service."

"Like what?"

"Well," Holden said. "He was some athlete. In his senior year in high school he was the captain of the football team and the track team. The football team won fourteen games straight and was the state champion. Luke was pretty generally recognized as the best running back in the state. At Tucson, he played the second half of the game with a broken collar bone and scored the winning touchdown in the fourth quarter with a plunge right over the center of the line from five yards out."

Hartney shook his head, but not in disbelief.

Holden went on. "There's more. The doctor worked last year as a company doctor for Phillips Dodge at the New Cornelia Mine at Ajo in southern Arizona. One of Frank's older brothers has a store there and when Frank graduated from High School he went down and stayed with his brother and worked in the mine to toughen himself up before he was called to flight training."

"Where Frank learned to fight or how the whole thing ever got organized the doctor didn't know, but on the Fourth of July, Frank was scheduled to fight five rounds with a Mexican for a purse of six hundred dollars, winner take all. The Mexican was a tough, hard rock miner about thirty years of age and he had won a similar fight the year before. All the Mexicans bet on him and the Anglos all had their money on Luke. The doctor said there must have been close to twenty thousand dollars bet."

"The fight was scheduled for eight o'clock in the evening, but it was 118 degrees that day and at eight o'clock it was still 110. They waited an hour and the temperature had only gone down five degrees, so they waited another hour. Finally at ten o'clock, the miners were tired of waiting and started to get rowdy so there was nothing to do but get on with the fight even though the temperature was still above a hundred."

"The Mexican came out swinging and in the first round he knocked Luke down three times and the last time, Luke was only saved by the bell. In the second round the Mexican sailed right in and tried to finish Luke off, but Luke managed to stay away from him and the Mexican, more or less, punched himself out. Toward the end of the round, Luke got in a couple of good shots of his own. In the third round, Luke got his second wind and knocked the Mexican down twice. When they rang the bell to start the fourth round the Mexican couldn't get up off his stool and his corner had to throw in the towel."

"I'll be a son of a bitch," Hartney said. "When I heard about what happened the first night Luke came to the squadron, I thought that somehow he had seen through O'Donnel's bluff, but now, hearing your story, I'd be willing to bet that he didn't."

"No question about it," Holden said. "He fell for O'Donnel's act just like every other new pilot he pulled it on, but Luke didn't care if O'Donnel was the heavy weight champion of New York state or Jack Dempsy's sparring partner. I don't think he would have backed down if it had been Jack Dempsy himself. But Luke must have figured, that as big as O'Donnel was, if he was to have any chance at all he would have to get in one real good punch at the start. When O'Donnel didn't get up, Luke must have been the most surprised man in the room."

"Damn," Hartney said. "I wish I had known all of this when he first came to the squadron."

"What difference would it have made?" Holden asked.

"I would have sent him to Rick before it became a problem."

"Why is it a problem now?" Holden said. "Both squadrons are under your command. Just transfer him over."

"It's not that simple," Hartney said.

"The court martial thing, you mean. Tell Grant to forget it."

"I can't do that," Hartney said. "I can't take away Grant's authority just to make things easy for Luke."

Captain Holden said nothing.

Hartney hesitated. Clearly, he needed to explain his dilemma to someone. Just as clearly, he was reluctant to do so. Finally he spoke. "George," he said. "This war can't go on for much longer. Now that you Americans are here in force there is no way that the Germans can win. Everything that we hear from intelligence indicates that the German economy is on the verge of collapse. There's been a poor harvest and coal production is way off because of the men that have been taken out of the mines to fight at the front. The war could be over by Christmas."

"I've heard that," Holden said.

"That being the case," Hartney went on. "The next war is more important than the present one."

"Next war?" Holden asked incredulously. "After the blood bath of the last four years you can't seriously believe that anyone would be insane enough to start another war?"

"Here in Europe, no," Hartney answered. "But in the Pacific, things still have to be decided."

"Things decided?"

"Yes," Hartney said. "The Japanese are an island nation, just like Britain. But unlike Britain, they don't have any colonies to supply them with raw materials and food and to buy the products of their factories. In the next ten or twenty years they are going to have to make a move to acquire those colonies and when they do it will mean war."

"War with who?"

"They've already beaten the Russians," Hartney said. "But I don't think there's much of value to them in Siberia. They need things like rice and oil and rubber and iron ore and tin. That would seem to indicate Malaya or Indonesia."

"They would take on the British Navy?"

"Not only the British, but the Americans as well, if Colonel Mitchell is correct. And he obviously has thought a lot about it. He thinks that the Japanese will open the war with a surprise air attack on Honolulu and Manila."

"From where? Hawaii must be a thousand miles from the nearest land." Holden said.

"From the decks of ships, if you believe Mitchell," Hartney said.

"Can they do that?"

"Theoretically," Hartney answered. "If you could put a platform the size of a football field on top of a hull, there isn't any reason why you couldn't operate pursuits off of it in good weather. The ship could always turn directly into the wind and could even run into the wind to shorten the take off and landing distance."

"What happens if the planes come back and the ship is sunk?" Holden asked.

"Good question," Hartney said. "I'll ask Colonel Mitchell about that the next time he gets started on his theory of how air power will win the next war."

"You mean he's worked out some theory about all of this?" Holden asked.

"I don't know if you could actually call it a theory," Hartney said. "But he has made some intriguing predictions."

"Like what?"

"Well, for instance, he has stated that aircraft dropping five hundred or thousand pounds bombs could sink a battle ship. If they could, it would mean that no battle ship could come within a hundred miles of the coast of any country having heavy bombing type aircraft."

"I'd have to see it to believe it."

"Believe this then," Hartney said. "It won't be long before we will have developed four engine bombers capable of carrying a payload of a ton of bombs a distance of two or three hundred miles. Imagine a dozen bombers, all bunched in a tight formation, letting their bombs go all at once on a target like an oil refinery or an armament works. Nothing will be safe from such an attack. It will change the whole science of warfare."

"And you think that all this will come to pass?" Captain Holden had become not only interested, but half way convinced.

"Maybe not exactly the way I have described it," Hartney said. "But air power is still in its infancy. There are going to be better planes and bigger planes and faster planes, you can be sure of that. But planes alone won't do it. Pilots are going to have to be trained and new tactics developed. A whole new branch of the armed forces will have to come into being so that when the next war comes we will be better prepared than we were this time."

Holden shrugged. "Interesting theory, but who's going to pay for it all? When the war is over the boys will come sailing home, the Army will discharge them and congress will cut expenditures back to a peace time level."

"Now George," Hartney said. "You've put your finger on it. Money is going to be tight. We're going to have to get the most out of every dollar. That means management and dedication over a lot of years. Do you think Luke or Rickenbacker will be willing to spend ten or twenty years, going six and eight years between promotions, working on new planes and new tactics on a shoe-string budget, just so that when the next war comes the Air Service will be ready."

"Not likely," Holden said.

"No," Hartney said. "But Captain Grant will. And he will be perfect for the job. He's an outstanding pilot, he has a lot of combat experience, he's an excellent manager and he will be well qualified to evaluate new aircraft and tactics."

"In spite of the fact that he's as yellow as a ripe banana."

Hartney scowled. "I'll let that pass, this time, on the basis that it was said between old friends, but I won't hear it again."

"Sorry." Holden looked down at his shoes.

There was a long period of silence, neither man willing to say any more and yet both aware that the conversation was not quite over. Hartney finally spoke. "George, you were here the night that Luke and Wehner went to Etain and got a balloon there and a Fokker apiece and Luke got another balloon at Bibinville. Wehner had engine trouble and had to land at a field just over the lines. When Luke landed he couldn't wait to get rearmed and refueled to go back for a third balloon he had seen. But his plane had been hit and there was oil running out of the bottom of his cowling. He begged Grant to give him another ship and Grant refused and Luke turned to me and I ordered Grant to give him his plane."

"I remember," Holden said. "He found the balloon by the light of the moon and burned it about eight o'clock at night. Grant got his airplane back without a scratch on it."

"There's more to it than that," Hartney said. "Grant took me into his office and asked me point blank why I had undermined his authority in front of most of his officers. The only thing I could tell him was that when a man wants to fight, you sometimes have to let him, that or break his spirit and have him refuse to fight when you want him to. But it works the other way too. When a man wants to establish some discipline in his squadron you some-times have to let him, that or break his spirit so that he'll never amount to much. I've gone about as far with Luke as I can. Now he's going to have to work things out with Grant on his own. If I interfere with Grant at this point I run the risk of driving out of the Air Service a man that could influence the outcome of the next war to a far greater extent than Luke and Rickenbacker together will influence the outcome of this one."

"If that's the case," Holden said thoughtfully. "I don't envy you your position. Luke isn't about to knuckle under for Grant. In fact, with Whener gone, he's going to be harder to control than ever. The first disagreement he has with Grant, he's going to go right over Grant's head and come to you. And the hardest part of that will be that Luke will probably be in the right."

"I know it," Hartney said resignedly. "I've got myself in a cor-ner where I can't seem to do a damned thing with either Grant or Luke. All I can do is hope that the war ends before things get completely out of hand.

Chapter 15

☆ ☆ ☆

When Luke returned to Rembercourt it was late on the evening of September 27th. He went directly to the barracks and was surprised to find in his room a Second Lieutenant sitting on Joe Wehner's bed, writing a letter.

"Who are you?" Luke demanded.

"Sir," the Lieutenant jumped to his feet. "I'm Lieutenant Roberts, one of the replacement pilots, I've been assigned to room with you." He held out his hand and Luke took it.

"Sir," the lieutenant started to go on.

Luke interrupted him. "Wait, my name is Frank. If you'll tell me yours, we can call each other by name."

"John Roberts and Sir, I mean Frank, I'd like the chance to fly with you the next time you go after a balloon."

"Well," Luke was clearly taken by surprise. "We'll see; you'll have to talk to Captain Grant or Vasconcelles about that."

"I have asked Captain Vasconcelles and he said it would be up to you," Roberts said.

"In that case, I'll talk to Vasconcelles and see if we can't work something out."

"Thank you Sir," Roberts hesitated. "I'm sorry, I mean Frank. I've just been writing to my parents to say that I'm rooming with you."

Luke smiled and threw his things on his bed. "I'll be back in while. I just need to check on some things."

Luke went out and across to the officer's mess and asked for Vasconcelles. Someone remembered that he was working late in operations so Luke got a schooner of beer and walked over to see him.

Grant and the clerks were all gone and only Vasconcelles was there going over the flight schedule for the following day. He looked up when the door opened and when he saw Luke, he got up and went over toward him and held out his hand. "Hey Frank, good to have you back."

They shook hands. "Hartney tells me that you almost bagged the old gray fox himself," Vasconcelles said, sitting back down.

"Jerry, I could have had him if I hadn't been so impatient."

"How's that?" Vasconcelles took a puff of his cigar.

"I didn't think that they would run when the first man went down. If I had known they would, I would have waited my turn for a crack at Udet."

"Smart move on his part Frank. He who fights and runs away, lives to fight another day."

"I wouldn't have run," Luke said.

"Sometimes it's the smartest thing to do," Vasconcelles said. "Though I have to admit that it goes against the grain with me. It's too easy to get into the habit."

"I guess," Luke said. Grant's name was never spoken, but they both gave his office door a knowing look.

"Talked to Grant yet?" Vasconcelles said.

"Just on the phone."

"What did he say."

"Told me to get back to Rembercourt and that when I arrived I was restricted to the base."

"No wonder it took you all day to get here," Vasconcelles laughed. "You want to lead a patrol in the morning?"

"I'm grounded too," Luke said.

"Bad as all that?"

"I can wait," Luke said. "Mitchell will want a balloon taken down in the next day or two and Grant will call my number."

"Speaking of balloons," Vasconcelles said. "We did one while you were gone."

"That so?" Luke said. "Who got it."

"A new Lieutenant, Roberts is his name, and I split the credit," Vasconcelles said. "I flew your Spad with the elephant gun loaded full tracer and he had both Vickers guns loaded with tracer. We went in side by side the way you and Wehner used to do and it flamed on our first pass. I'm not sure I would have wanted to make any more. The fire really comes up from the ground and you have to sit real still so that all your rounds strike in a tight pattern."

"I know."

"I guess you would," Vasconcelles conceded.

"This Roberts any good?" Luke asked.

"He came to us from Issouden with some of the highest marks they have ever given. Grant flew his indoctrination ride and thought he was pretty good. So far, he's volunteered for everything that's come up and he's done everything that we asked of him." Vasconcelles said.

"He wants to fly with me." Luke said.

"You could do worse for a wing man, although he isn't any Joe Wehner; at least not yet. He isn't afraid to mix it up though. That's half of it right there."

"Set it up then, if you can." Luke said.

Vasconcelles nodded.

"See you in the morning," Luke said as he let himself out the door.

The next day dawned bright and clear and Luke and the other pilots were up early and down to the flight line by the time the sun began to rise above the trees at the end of the field. A dawn patrol led by Grant had already gone off and four more Spads had been rolled out and run up so as to be ready for an immediate take off. The pilots not flying came over to Luke in twos and threes and expressed their sympathy over Wehner and their congratulations over his victory over one of Udet's best pilots.

Since the night that he had landed soaked with gasoline and the other pilots had come for him and Wehner with a bottle of champagne, things had changed. Luke was a not only a member of the squadron in good standing, but as the American Ace of Aces and the one whose victories had put the 27th ahead of Rickenbacker's Hat in the Ring Squadron, the unofficial leader as well. The 27th had been designated as a balloon buster squadron and several more aircraft were being outfitted with the French 45 caliber elephant gun that Luke had introduced. Luke's entire morning was taken up with unofficial briefings on the art of balloon strafing and discussions about the finer points of maneuvering against the smaller and lighter Fokker.

Grant's flight landed without having seen any enemy planes and Grant acknowledged Luke's presence with only a curt, "good morning." Nothing was said about when Luke might fly again. The afternoon passed without much activity and then, a little after five thirty, a call came down from Group about a balloon near Bontheville that was directing artillery fire on to an American supply column. The sky was clear and the moon would be bright enough for the balloon to direct artillery fire all night. Mitchell wanted the balloon down as soon as possible, but daylight was fast fading away.

"Frank," Vasconcelles came out of operations with a map in his hand. "We've got an errand for you to run before supper."

"Is it cleared upstairs?" Luke wanted to know.

Vasconcelles nodded. He laid his map out beside Luke's and they marked the position of the balloon and considered possible routes. "What about escorts?" Luke asked.

"Grant would prefer none, but I can give you four if you want."

"Maybe Grant would like to fly it without any covering flight."

"Frank, you don't have to go if you don't want to." Vasconcelles said. "I only asked because I thought you'd want it. Just shake your head and I'll send someone else."

"No," Luke said. "I wouldn't give Grant the satisfaction of scheduling a mission that I wouldn't fly." He looked around at a cloudless, darkening sky. "Just give me Roberts. Put him in one of the new Spads with an elephant gun and arm both the Vickers and the 45s with full tracer."

An orderly ran down the line with the orders for the armament and Luke took Roberts aside for a quick briefing. "Look," he told him. "Here's where the balloon is, just this side of the road junction with the railroad coming in above. The town is just below it."

Roberts nodded.

"Now," Luke continued. "I expect that there will be Fokkers over the balloon at four or five thousand feet. If there was any cloud cover we'd try to sneak in low under it, but since there isn't any, we'll come in high. You just follow me at a couple of hundred yards. If there are any Fokkers up at all, we'll make just the one pass and then dive for home."

Roberts nodded again.

"Don't worry about saving ammunition. If I don't burn it, fire as soon as you're in range and keep firing until you're right on it."

They ran out to the two Spads that had been started and were running with mechanics holding on to the wings. As soon as Roberts signaled that he was ready, Luke pushed the power up and they were quickly airborne and turning for the lines.

They climbed out at a steady rate, keeping to the allied side of the lines. The plan that Luke had been turning over in his mind began to jell. They would make it look like an ordinary evening patrol, just taking that last look before darkness really fell. Then when they were at eight thousand feet and he had marked where the balloon should be, they would dive across the line, drop quickly through any Fokkers that were patrolling, take one shot each at the balloon and, whether they had burned it or not, keep on diving at their maximum rate until they were back on the allied side of the trenches.

They reached no-man's-land and turned to the southeast. The sky above them was light and clear of any aircraft. Below them, the ground was beginning to darken. Luke looked at the map with the flashlight that was now a standard part of his equipment and searched the enemy side of the lines for the road junction outside of Bontheville. Roberts held his position off to one side and a little back.

They passed what Luke was certain was the road junction and went on for another minute before they slowly turned around. He had not seen the balloon, but he did not expect to until he was almost upon it. He hoped that Roberts could shoot. At the speed that they were going to attack, he might be able to do little more than to mark the target.

At last they were back opposite the road junction and he rocked his wings and pointed down. Roberts rocked his wings in acknowledgment. Luke pushed his Spad over and started down at about a forty-five degree angle. He wondered if Roberts had remembered to close his radiator shutters to keep the engine from cooling in the long dive.

The wind was soon screaming in the wires. Looking back he saw Roberts following as briefed. He concentrated on the spot where the balloon should be, looking for a smooth dark shape against the irregular landscape.

He passed through five thousand feet without a sign of the balloon or of any Fokkers. And then the shape appeared, still a good thousand feet below him. He rolled to the right almost 45 degrees to bring his guns to bear and prepared to fire. It was then that he saw the Fokkers off to the west They were at least a quarter of a mile away. They could never catch them, not at the speed that they were diving.

As yet there were no muzzle flashes from the ground. They had achieved complete surprise. He steadied the sight on the nose of the balloon and started both guns running. The tracers went home and in a matter of seconds the nose of the balloon was burning. He rolled toward the lines and looked back for Roberts.

In stark contrast against the light sky he saw a single Spad turning back against a half dozen Fokkers. "No!" he shouted. "Dive for home with me!" It was no use. He pulled his Spad back over in a half loop as hard as he dared and rolled out, still climbing with the excess speed he had built up in the dive. Roberts and the Fokkers were closing and he was still to far away to be of any help.

"Dive!" he shouted again. "Dive away toward me!"

It was too late. A shower of tracers filled the air and the Spad burst into flames and began to spiral toward the ground. The Fokkers turned toward Luke and with the odds so heavy against him he had no choice except to dive back toward his own lines. A few tracers went by his right wing and then the Fokkers fell far behind and abandoned the chase.

He crossed the darkness of no-man's-land unable to understand what had happened. Roberts had specific instructions to stay with him and he had known that they were to make a single pass at the balloon and then cross back over the lines. What had caused Roberts to turn back into the Fokkers, he would never know.

He turned his flashlight on to the compass on the floor and set a course for Rembercourt. In less than a minute the familiar signal of a green flare followed by two red ones appeared on the horizon just over his gunsight.

He thought of the night that Colonel Mitchell had come to dine with them, when he and Wehner had burned three balloons in a little more than a minute. They had come home to the same signal of a green followed by two reds that night. But there would be no celebration when he landed this time. Only questions that he could not answer about what had happened to Roberts.

He shined the flashlight on the compass again and set a new course for the Storks.

Chapter 16

It was the morning of September 29th. Hartney, once again found himself at Rembercourt trying to make peace between Grant and Luke. Luke had spent the night at the Storks and now, Grant claimed, was refusing to return. Luke had called the night before and told Vasconcelles about Roberts and had said that he was having an engine problem that might delay his return.

Grant had tried to talk to Luke on the phone, but the answer he invariably got was that Luke's whereabouts were unknown or that he was flying his Spad, testing an engine adjustment.

"As if it wasn't bad enough when he lied," Grant said. "Now he's got the god damned frogs lying for him. I tell them to place him under arrest and they tell me that there not sure that he is still on their field."

"Arrest, Al, isn't that going a little far," Hartney said.

"What else can I do?" Grant said. "That boy isn't subject to ordinary military discipline. I want him back here and if I can't get him any other way, I'll send the military police and have them bring him back in handcuffs and leg irons. I've made it clear to their base commander that if Luke hasn't left by noon, I'll send the military police for him and I'll expect the full cooperation of the French authorities."

"Oh, Al," Hartney said shaking his head. "Are you really sure you want to do that. Do you honestly want both of you in a position where neither one can back down or give an inch."

"God damn it, Major," Grant said. "I've got a squadron to run here. I can't spend all day, every day, wondering what the hell Luke will be up to next. Since he's been here he's been more damned trouble that all of the rest of the squadron put together."

"Al," Hartney said quietly. "Since he's been here he's had more victories than all the rest of the squadron put together."

"You always take his side, don't you?" Grant said bitterly.

"I'd like to think we're all on the same side."

Grant ignored that remark and went on, "What the hell is there over at the Storks that has such a big attraction for Luke, anyway?"

"We ought to go over some day and see," Hartney said. "Maybe they have some kind of non-military discipline that works out better in a pursuit squadron."

"Hah," Grant said. "Those frogs don't have any organization at all. They couldn't organize a piss line in a brewery. If I wanted advice on how to run a pursuit squadron I sure as hell wouldn't look to them. The Germans, maybe; the French or the British, never."

"Well," Hartney said. "We can refight the war after it's over. What can I do right now to help you out with Luke?"

"Nothing," Grant said. "Absolutely nothing. Keep out of it and let me handle him."

"All right," Hartney said. "I'll go on back to Group Headquarters. I've got plenty of work to do there. Just do me one favor, Al. Give me a call when you know whether Luke is coming back or whether you're going to have to send someone for him. I won't interfere. I just want to know."

"I can do that," Grant said.

Hartney went out to the field where his Spad was parked. They had laid out a runway just down the road from Group Headquarters and he was now able to fly back and forth from his squadrons when the weather was good.

Ten minutes after noon, Grant called Hartney to tell him that Luke had departed the Storks and was headed for Rembercourt. Much relieved, Hartney went to lunch. No sooner had he returned than his phone rang again. It was Vasconcelles calling from the temporary forward field that they often used when they were expecting enemy photographic flights.

Luke had landed only a few minutes before and wanted to be refueled so that he could go and look for balloons. Vasconcelles had left early that morning, so had no idea of what had passed between Grant and Hartney, but he was not about to release Luke for a solo flight across the lines on his own authority. Vasconcelles had tried to reach Grant, but Grant had just taken off on a combat patrol and might be gone for an hour or more.

Hartney was furious when he heard the news. "Do you have a pistol with you?" he demanded of Vasconcelles.

Vasconcelles did.

"Then," Hartney said. "You tell Luke that he is not to be refueled or to take off until I get there. If he makes any attempt to leave, put four or five bullets into his radiator. Have I made myself clear?"

"Yes sir," was all that Vasconcelles could manage before the line was cut off. He wondered what the hell Luke had done this time. He would find out soon enough.

Hartney landed some thirty minutes later and taxied his Spad up to an abandoned hanger where it could be pushed out of sight. Vasconcelles and Luke were waiting for him.

"Now what the hell is going on?" Hartney demanded of Luke. "Why aren't you at Rembercourt like you promised Grant?"

"I started for there," Luke said. "But then I saw this two seater, way up high, flying back and forth along the lines. I thought it might be a German ship, so I climbed up to investigate. I had to go to almost fifteen thousand feet to get to it and then it turned out to be one of ours. I got a little dizzy then from the altitude and I let down, but I couldn't seem to get my bearings. When I saw the field here, I had only a little fuel left and I thought I had better land. I just wanted to get refueled."

"Enough," Hartney said. "If you can't tell a better story than that, don't make the effort."

Luke hung his head and said nothing.

"Go on and get your Spad refueled and then come back here," Hartney told him.

Luke went off.

"Jerry, what the hell are we going to do with him?" Hartney asked of Vasconcelles.

"I don't know, Harold. What do you want to do?"

"I want to make him a team player and a part of the squadron. I want to get him out of Grant's hair. That's what I want."

"Well, I've got a suggestion for you, Harold." It was clear from the way he spoke that Vasconcelles and Hartney had known each other very well at some point in the war. "You send Grant up to

Issouden as an instructor, you make me the new squadron commander and I appoint Luke as my executive officer. Everybody's
happy and I have a squadron that will outscore Rickenbacker's two
to one."

"You don't mean it."

"Yes I do, but you won't consider it."

"No I won't. Especially the part about Luke as an executive officer."

"Short sighted on your part," Vasconcelles said. "You want Luke
to show a little responsibility, give him some responsibility. Holden
told me what he found out about Luke. The kid's a natural leader,
so let him lead. You combine what I know with what he can do and
we'll roll up Udet and his Jagstaffel like a cheap mattress. What's
more, we'll bring the whole squadron along with us."

"You're serious, aren't you?"

"You're damned right I am. I see a squadron that's desperate for
some leadership and I see a kid that can lead by example being
pushed aside because he doesn't fit somebody's idea of what an
officer ought to be. You tell me where there's any sense in that."

"But Luke doesn't know the meaning of the word discipline,"
Hartney protested. "It's like Grant says, 'he's uncontrollable.'"

"That's where you're wrong," Vasconcelles cut him off. "Grant
is the one that's uncontrollable. The day that he gave Luke his
check ride and had to land with a string of laundry hanging from
one wing and Luke sitting with his prop ten feet behind his tail, he
never said a word to Frank. He just sulked off to his quarters and
then went to town and didn't come back until morning. If it had
been me or you and some kid fresh out of Issouden had managed
to get on our tail and we couldn't shake him, he wouldn't have got
the switches and the fuel turned off before we were over to his
plane to slap him on the back and offer our congratulations. But I
guess you didn't hear about what happened or you would have said
something to Grant."

"I heard about it," Hartney conceded. "But too late to want to
make an issue out of it."

"What about his first combat report that Grant threw into the
dirt outside of operations. Called Luke a liar in front of a dozen
other pilots. What kind of discipline or leadership is that?" The
greenest ninety day wonder out of Officer's Candidate School
knows that you praise in public and criticize in private."

"I spoke to him about that. I wanted to believe Luke, but Grant convinced me that his story about the Hannoveraner was a complete fabrication from beginning to end."

"You still think that?"

"Of course not," Hartney said.

"But you haven't said anything to Grant?"

"No. I've taken Luke's side in too many arguments to bring up one more thing that's over and done with."

"What about last night?" Vasconcelles insisted. "Grant's been saying that Roberts was killed because Luke ran off and left him just like he did Wehner and that he went to the Storks because he didn't have the courage to admit that to Grant."

"You actually heard him say that?"

"In the mess this morning, just before we left to come up here." Vasconcelles said. "The truth of the matter is that Roberts disobeyed Luke's order to make only one diving pass and then to keep on diving for our lines. The only thing that Frank can figure out is that Roberts thought he was good enough to take on a half dozen Fokkers all by himself or that he thought that if he engaged the Fokkers, Frank would come back into the fight to help him. Frank did try to climb back up to help Roberts, but before he could get close, Roberts was already on fire. All alone with all those Fokkers above him, Frank had no choice but to dive for our lines."

"Well, that does it," Hartney said. "I'm going to have to make some changes. Not the ones you want, I can't send Grant to Issouden until a director's job opens up there. It would be degrading for him to go simply as an instructor. But I can send Luke there as an instructor, or as a special lecturer, if you will. Then, when I can move Grant, you can have Luke back. I won't promise that he will carry the title of executive officer, but you can use him any way you see fit."

"Don't wait too long," Vasconcelles answered. "I've got some new ideas that I want to try, but I need a shooter like Luke for a clean up hitter. I wouldn't want the war to end without seeing what he could do with the kind of organized backup that Richtoffen had."

"I won't wait," Hartney reassured him. "I'll have Luke at Issouden before the sun sets tomorrow and then we'll see what I can do for you. If I can't move Grant, there is the possibility that we will form a third squadron. If we do, it will be yours and you can have Luke for the asking. For now, that's the best I can offer."

"Well, that pretty well takes care of tomorrow," Vasconcelles said. "Now all we have to worry about is what we are going to do about tonight."

"Tonight?" Hartney said. "What about tonight?"

"We got a report, just before you landed, about three new German balloons that have been put up between Dun-sur-Muse and Dulcon. Frank wanted to go after them right away, but I told him that he would have to wait until evening."

"I don't think we should let him go," Hartney said. "Grant, after all, did ground him. And after what happened last night, we can expect that there may be a dozen or more Fokkers up."

"How do you propose to stop him?" Vasconcelles ventured.

"What do you mean?"

"Dun-sur-Muse is only five minutes from here. We've already plotted it out on the map. If you let Frank take off, he'll go after them just as sure as hell."

"Not if I order him to return with the rest of us."

"Don't be too sure," Vasconcelles cautioned him. "You'd be giving an order that you had no way of enforcing. You can see how much luck Grant has had in getting him back to Rembercourt."

"He wouldn't disobey me," Hartney insisted.

"I wouldn't put it to the test," Vasconcelles said. "Not today. Grant is the one who ordered him back to Rembercourt. You'd only be restating Grant's original order."

"We'll unload his guns then. Then he won't have any choice but to go back to Rembercourt."

Vasconcelles shook his head. "What if a half dozen Fokkers drop down on us just as we're coming off the ground. I can see the headlines in the American papers now. LUKE KILLED WITH EMPTY GUNS. AMERICAN ACE DIES AS A RESULT OF DISCIPLINARY ACTION."

"Not likely," Hartney countered. " And even if we did run into Fokkers, none of them would ever get on Frank's tail."

"I'll tell you what is likely then," Vasconcelles said. "Luke will fly to the Storks and get his guns armed there. Then he'll come back in the dark and find those balloons and burn them, or die trying. The only way you can stop him is to place him under arrest and send him back on one of the trucks with the mechanics. Even then I'd put those four or five bullet holes into the radiator of his Spad because, if I know Frank, he'll find a way to escape and come back here and go after those balloons, even if it's after midnight."

"Jesus Christ," Hartney said. "How did we ever get ourselves into a corner like this?"

Vasconcelles did not answer. He had made his point.

Finally, Hartney said, "If I let him go, what are the chances that he could pull it off and get back to here or Rembercourt?"

"Good," Vasconcelles said. "If he'd be content to bag one balloon like he did last night and then run for home. But that isn't Frank's style. He'll want all three and he'll keep trying until he gets them or runs out of ammunition."

"You think they'll be laying for him?"

"I'm sure of it. Three balloons like that, evenly spaced in a straight line. It's a deliberate trap. As soon as the first one flames, the Fokkers will all dive for the second. Coming or going, some of them are going to be in a position to get a shot at Frank."

Hartney walked out of the hanger and Vasconcelles followed him. They looked at the high clouds that were moving in from the west. It was only four o'clock, but already the clouds were beginning to hide the sun. It would be dark early that night.

Luke came up to them. He was smiling. "I'm fueled now and both guns are loaded full tracer. I can leave any time."

Hartney and Vasconcelles looked at each other. It was hard for them to believe that this bright faced, school boy was not only the terror of the German balloon corps, but of the American Air Command as well.

Vasconcelles gave a kind of a shrug and looked back to the west. He had said his piece and now it was between Hartney and Luke.

"Frank," Hartney said. "We think that this may be a kind of trap that the Germans have deliberately laid. We haven't as yet had a request to bring those balloons down. Maybe we ought to let them go this time."

"Major," Luke protested. "It's dead certain that they'll want them down tomorrow. And then we'll have to go after them in broad daylight and lose all chance of crossing the lines without being seen. Dun-sur-Muse is only five minutes from here. The Germans don't know that we have any planes on this field. If they are looking for an attack tonight they'll be expecting it to come from Rembercourt. I can take off and burn all three before a plane from Rembercourt could even get to the first one. This is too good a chance to pass."

Hartney hesitated. He had a lot of arguments against Luke's going, but he realized that Vasconcelles was right. Unless he put Luke under arrest and took him back to Rembercourt by truck,

Luke would find a way to attack those balloons.

"How would you plan to do it?" Hartney asked.

"Go in low, right in the tree tops where I can see the balloons and any Fokkers against the sky. The first balloon will be there at Dun, right across from the bend in the Meuse. I'll go right down the line and make only one pass on each balloon, whether I burn it or not, and then I'll turn and come back the way I came, right in the tree tops. If any Fokkers want to come down there with me in the dark, they're welcome."

"Do you want one of us to come with you as cover?"

"No." Luke's jaw set and the bright blue eyes suddenly turned a steely gray. "No more escorts."

Chapter 17

☆ ☆ ☆

Vasconcelles stood by as Luke buckled himself into his Spad. It had been run up by the mechanics ten minutes before and was ready to go. It was still in the abandoned hanger out of sight of any German planes that might come over.

"Frank," Vasconcelles said. "I can't tell you what to do. Too much depends on what you find when you get there. But the ground batteries and any Fokkers that are up will all be expecting you to start at one end of the line or the other. If it looks like some kind of a trap, you might surprise them by taking the center balloon first and then just diving for our lines the way you did last night."

Luke nodded and pointed at the clock in the Spad that was coming up on five o'clock. "I know it's a little early, but I want to get started now . The light on the ground is fading fast."

Vasconcelles raised his hand and made a turning motion in the air. In front of the second hanger where the other Spads were waiting, Hartney nodded his approval.

"O.K. Frank," he said. "It's all your show."

The mechanics pulled the prop through and the engine caught. Luke ran the power up and the instruments quickly moved into the normal range.

"We'll put up a green and two reds, same as always, here and at Rembercourt," Vasconcelles shouted above the noise of the engine.

Luke nodded and waved away the mechanics who were holding the wing tips. The power came full on and the Spad roared out of the hanger and onto the field. In seconds it was up and headed for the Meuse. Three other Spads that had come up with Vasconcelles that morning took off and headed back for Rembercourt. Hartney and Vasconcelles remained to await Luke's return.

A minute later a Spad, no more than twenty feet above the ground, crossed the American observation post at Souilly and dropped a note that read, 'Watch for balloons on the Meuse - Luke.' The watch commander immediately picked up the field phone and relayed the message to all the American observation posts in the area. The information quickly spread up and down the lines. At the magic words, 'Luke is up,' thousands of men put down mess kits, letters, reports, whatever they were about, came out of their dugouts and mounted up on the fire steps of their trenches to gaze at the rapidly darkening eastern horizon.

Luke crossed the Meuse with his wheels skimming the water and quickly spotted the balloon that was moored just outside of Dun. He turned to set up a firing pass down the length of the balloon and checked the sky above him. There were four Fokkers almost directly overhead and another four a couple of hundred yards behind them. They gave no indication that they had seen him.

Fokkers first and then the balloons, he thought, and began to climb so as to come up behind the last flight. When he reached the level of the balloon though, it looked too big and too tempting to pass. The Fokkers still seemed unaware of his presence and there was no fire coming up from the ground. There was just time to take it right out from under their noses.

A shallow turn to the left brought the balloon into his gunsight and he began firing as soon as he was within range. Two dozen rounds went home and a flame suddenly flared at the point of impact. It was getting easy.

He looked for the Fokkers then. They had drifted behind and to one side of him, but they had seen the flames and they were diving for him. He pushed the stick forward and forced his Spad down below the huge, burning bag of gas. He passed under the nose, just missing the forward mooring cables, and continued diving along the length of it. The two observers, descending in parachutes, stared at Luke with unbelieving eyes as he went by. If the ground batteries saw him, they were too astonished to fire.

At the tail of the balloon he stood the Spad up on the left wing and made a diving turn that carried him back under the now falling giant. All above him was an almost blinding mass of flames. Pieces of burning silk fell all around him. He had barely passed out from under the nose when the entire balloon dropped, still burning, on to the support winch.

He turned hard to the left again and looked for the Fokkers. Four were above and ahead of him. Two were trailing them and the last two were directly above him not more than fifty feet away. The turn under the burning balloon had thrown them off completely. They had no idea where he was.

He eased his Spad up behind the last two Fokkers and took dead aim on the fuel tank of the one on the left hand side. He was too close to miss and to save ammunition he fired only a half dozen rounds from the Vickers gun.

The Fokker flamed immediately and before the other could react, Luke flamed it as well. The remaining six Fokkers turned away to the north and he turned after them. He followed them for almost a minute, but they were climbing away from him and even at full power he was slowly falling behind.

The second balloon appeared to his left then and he turned back toward it. The Fokkers were no longer a threat. They had had all they wanted and were still climbing away to the north when he looked back for the last time.

He started his approach on the second balloon. This time there was no surprise. The ground batteries opened up when he was still far out of firing range. The ground was a solid sheet of flame and he could hear the guns above the noise of his engine. The Spad lurched from side to side as the ground fire tore first at one wing and then the other.

He blocked out the noise and the gun flashes and brought his sight to bear on the back of the balloon. A dozen rounds from each of his guns at the maximum range produced no effect. He pressed on through a hail of fire that ripped and tore at the fabric of his Spad. Finally, when he was less than a hundred yards away, he fired again and this time flames shot out of the nose of the balloon.

He pulled up and passed almost directly over the top of the dying mammoth. The ground fire stopped for a moment and then, as he came clear of the tail, the Spad was hit by a barrage of fire that shook it as a dog might shake a rat. There was a hard blow to his back and then everything was black.

When he saw again, it was through a cloudy haze. The Spad was diving at a steep angle and the wings were tilted to the right. Instinct alone leveled the wings and brought the nose up to the horizon. He could not remember where he was or why he was there.

He put his left hand out of the cockpit to force some fresh air onto his face. The pain shot through his shoulder and neck with such force that he saw stars flashing before his eyes. His collar bone was broken. It was all right, he told himself, they could take him to the locker room and tape it up. He could play again in the second half.

He closed his eyes and took a deep breath and felt a dull pain deep in his chest. He needed to lie down for a few minutes and let his head clear. He still wasn't sure where he was or what he should do next.

The Spad was again violently rocked by ground fire and, when he looked up, there was directly in front of him a large gray shape against the sky. Instinctively, he pulled back on the stick and brought the gun sight up to cover the top edge. He fired both guns and flames licked out from where the tracers had gone in. He turned away to the left to avoid running into the shape and saw it blossom into a ball of fire as he went past.

The ground below him sparkled with flashes of light and something heavy slammed into the Spad. The roar of the engine stopped and the propeller windmilled along in a kind of hushed breathing as the Spad slowed and began to settle. The flashes of light and the noise of the guns fell away behind him as he descended almost to the tops of the tallest trees. Without knowing why he did it, he reached up and turned on the emergency tank in the upper wing.

The engine sputtered and then roared back into life. The sound and the vibration shook him back into some semblance of sense. He had to get home. But where was home?

His head began to clear. Home was there toward the west where the setting sun showed as an orange smudge in the heavy clouds. He turned in that direction and looked for a green or a red flare. The fuel in the emergency tank would only last for ten minutes. In that time he had to cross the lines and find a place to land.

The steeple of a church suddenly loomed up directly in front of him and he turned aside to see himself flying down the main street of a small town. Muzzles flashed from down in the street and he felt the Spad hit again. He dropped the nose and emptied his guns into the two bunches of soldiers that he could see. The tracers ricocheted off the cobblestones and the brick walls of the buildings and filled the darkening street with a shower of sparks. He saw several bodies tumbled off their feet.

He was past the town then and he added power to gain more

height, but the engine was not responding. A white mist streamed back from the radiator and he felt the sting of droplets of scalding water on his cheek. The engine revolutions continued to drop and somewhere in the engine there seemed to be something glowing red hot. There would be no returning across the lines that night.

Off to his left was a small meadow. He started a descending turn toward it and pulled the throttle to idle. At that, the engine froze and the propeller stopped dead. He turned off both fuel switches and the magnetos as the ground came up to meet him.

There was a bump and a short hop and then the Spad lurched to a stop, almost overturning in the rough, tussocky grass. There was no sound except that of water boiling and steam escaping from the damaged radiator.

Luke sat for almost a minute, trying to clear his head. He could not recall exactly when he had been hit, and was not certain whether it had been two or three balloons, but he remembered the first balloon and the two Fokkers one right after the other.

He undid his safety belt and carefully stood up on the seat of the Spad. Back in the direction from which he had come, he could see the cross on the church steeple and, below it, the lights of the town itself. He remembered shooting at the troops in the street.

A spell of dizziness caught him then and he was forced to sit down on the edge of the cockpit. In spite of the coolness of the night, he felt hot and he was sweating. His throat and mouth were dry and he wanted something to drink.

He took his 45 and eased himself out of the cockpit and on to the lower wing. The back of the cockpit was smeared with blood from his flying suit. He had been hit hard. He would need a doctor from the town to stop the bleeding. And he would need an attic room or a hayloft where he could rest for a few days before he was able to travel.

The sound of water boiling and steam escaping from the radiator stopped and he could hear the quiet murmur of a small stream running at the bottom of the meadow. He made his way down to it and drank from his cupped hands and splashed the cold water on to his head and face. The current swirled around his legs and spread out a fan shaped plume of his blood.

Beyond the meadow there was a deep woods. If he had not been hurt, he would have hidden himself in there and waited to see what the morning brought. But there was no way to wish away the pain in his chest and the blood on the water. He needed a doctor, by midnight at the latest.

He was trying to decide if it was dark enough for him to start for the town when he heard the sound of boots on gravel. A large number of men were coming out along the road from the town at double time. The Germans must have seen the Spad go down, or at least heard the engine quit, and they were coming to look for him.

They would not miss the plane, standing as it was, all alone in the middle of an open meadow. He needed to get away from it, but he could not afford to run and get his wound to bleeding more than it was. He forced himself to think. The big bucks never ran when they were hit. They holed up in the smallest piece of cover they could find and let the hunters walk past them.

Down the creek, not twenty yards away, was a small thicket. He eased himself into it and took some of the mud from the bank and smeared it onto his face and hands so that they would not show as white spots among the dark leaves. As soon as the Germans passed, he would try to sneak back toward the town. They would never expect him to move in that direction.

Up on the road the sound of boots on gravel stopped and he heard one of the soldiers cry out something in German. They had spotted the Spad and must have been able to see that the cockpit was empty.

He waited. There was the sound of orders given and then the sound of men moving cautiously through the meadow. He saw them when they reached his Spad. They took their time and looked it over carefully. He could hear them talking, the sound carrying clearly in the still night air. He wished they would hurry. In spite of the fact that he stood almost knee deep in cold water, he was burning up with fever.

The Germans seemed to be arguing about something. Finally, a voice with the sound of authority called out loudly, "Kammarad?" He made no answer and again it was repeated, "Kammarad?"

Surrender? Would they let him walk out with his hands in the air? Would they see to it that his wound was dressed by one of their surgeons? He doubted it. He had seen too many of their comrades go down in the street back there in the town.

"Kammarad!" The call came the third time as an order.

A hot, hard pain spread through Luke's chest and forced him to his knees. All the world spun before his eyes and he could hardly take a breath. When the pain passed he felt too weak to get to his feet. But he would not answer. He would get himself into town and find a doctor if he had to crawl on his hands and knees.

High overhead, through a break in the low clouds, he could see mare's tails turning pink and gold as they caught the last rays of the setting sun. On the ground, it grew ever darker. The soldiers around the Spad were talking again. With luck, they would give it up and come back in the morning.

It was not to be. The men spread out and began to work their way down toward the stream. They were looking for trouble. If they found him, they would get it. Whatever happened, he was not going to be dragged out to the road by the collar like some sneak thief and left to bleed to death in a ditch. He took the 45 from the pocket of his flight suit and pulled the slide back and slowly eased a round forward into the chamber.

It was beginning to get quite dark. He wished he had thought to have hidden himself somewhere by the side of the road that led back to the town. They were not looking for him there. Still, he was well concealed. They could easily walk past him in the fading light.

Two of them though, seemed to be headed straight for him. He brought the automatic up with both hands and steadied it at the chest of the first man. The men came on until they were little more than ten feet away. He held himself still and, in the dim light, they did not see him.

Off to his left, someone called out excitedly. He guessed that they had found his footprints in the mud along the bank of the stream. The men in front of him stopped and turned toward the voice and he thought that they might go off in that direction.

Then the one in front, a big man, looked back directly at Luke. He hesitated for a split second and then threw his rifle to his shoulder. Luke shot him before he could pull the trigger.

The second man leveled his rifle at Luke and Luke shot and missed. The muzzle of the rifle flashed and Luke heard the bullet rip through the leaves beside him. The man worked frantically at the bolt of his rifle. Luke steadied the automatic and shot the man before he could get off another round.

The shots gave his position away. From the meadow, volley after volley of rifle fire tore through the thicket, tearing and shredding the leaves. All of the shots passed over the head of Luke who had thrown himself down and lay in the stream with only his face and the 45 showing above the water. In a moment, orderss were shouted back and forth and the firing ceased.

The shooting started his wound bleeding again and, where moments before he had been burning with fever, Luke was shivering in the cold water. He had been forced to reveal his hiding place, but he had also shown them that he could bite. They wouldn't be so anxious now, to play hide and seek with him in the dark.

The pain in his chest had become bad, worse than anything he had ever known, but he had to move on. A hundred yards, he told himself. It was no more than a hundred yards to where the stream ran into a hedgerow. Once he was there he could rest for thirty minutes or so until it was completely dark. Then, another thirty minutes would take him back to one of the houses at the edge of town. He crawled on his stomach to keep his head below the top of the stream bank.

He had gone less than half way when, up on the meadow, he heard the sound of a number of men moving toward him. There were still six rounds left in the 45, but out in the open where he was, there was no chance for him in a fight. He hid himself against the bank of the stream and lay perfectly still with his face pressed into the mud and waited for the men to walk past.

The men came closer and finally Luke heard the sound of boots splashing in the water.

He never heard the sound of the shot that killed him.

Chapter 18

☆ ☆ ☆

At the forward field, Hartney and Vasconcelles saw the glow in the sky as Luke burned the first balloon at Dun. This information was quickly confirmed by a number of observers and passed along to the operations room at Rembercourt where the pilots of the 27th had gathered as soon as the news of Luke's single handed patrol had been announced. Missed by all of the observers was the downing of the two Fokkers, their small flaming descents no doubt lost in the blazing wreck of the falling balloon.

As Luke approached the second balloon the fire from the ground became so heavy that the sound of the guns was clearly heard in many of the front line trenches. Moments later, observers saw the glow of another burning balloon. This news was met by a cheer from all of the pilots and mechanics at Rembercourt. Hartney and Vasconcelles, at the forward field, only exchanged worried glances. They knew that Luke was on his way toward the third balloon.

The news of the third balloon burning set off another cheer at Rembercourt and brought a sigh of relief to all of the men at the forward field. Luke had done it again. Hartney noted the time on his watch. Luke's flying time from the location of the last balloon to the forward field was something less than fifteen minutes and Hartney wanted the first of the flares to go up in eight minutes.

The flares went up exactly on time and were repeated every minute. Fifteen minutes passed and then twenty and there was still no sound of an aircraft engine. Hartney and Vasconcelles could only hope that Luke had gone on to Rembercourt. When they queried Grant over the field phone he informed them that he had been putting up flares every minute for over ten minutes and that there was no sign of Luke.

An hour passed and it grew very dark and there was still no report of Luke. Neither Hartney nor Vasconcelles could bring himself to express what they knew must be true. Finally, two hours after the time that Luke had taken off, Hartney said, "That's it Jerry. His fuel would have run out by now. He's down somewhere."

Vasconcelles shrugged, trying to put the best face on the situation, "It won't be the first night that he's had to land in a field and get someone to give him a ride home."

Hartney talked to Grant at Rembercourt and alerted all the front line posts to the possibility that there might be a Spad down somewhere just over the lines or perhaps in no-man's-land. Then there was nothing to do but wait.

The night passed without any news and at dawn, Hartney and Vasconcelles took off and flew to Dun-sur-Meuse. There they found the Meuse and all the valleys that led into it covered with a heavy layer of fog. They turned back and headed for Rembercourt. As they dropped down over the field to check the wind direction before they landed they saw several dozen khaki colored bundles stacked against the side of the operations building. As they turned on to their final approach, the khaki colored bundles stood up and made their way to the flight line. They were the squadron mechanics who had spent the night there wrapped up in blankets and ponchos so that they might hear any news of Luke as soon as it came in.

Grant met Hartney and Vasconcelles at the flight line and reported that he was about to lead a flight of four on a low level sweep of the allied side of the lines in the area where Luke would have had to crossed had he been able to make it back. Colonel Mitchell had called and Hartney went into operations to return the call. Vasconcelles ordered the mechanics off to the mess hall before they caught their death of colds. The pilots all crowded around Vasconcelles for the latest news, but all he could tell them was that the Meuse and the surrounding country was covered with fog.

Grant's flight returned in little over an hour and reported that they had seen nothing. None of the balloon observers could see a Spad down anywhere in no-man's-land. By noon it was certain that Luke had come down somewhere on the German side of the lines.

Then, as had been the case when Joe Wehner went down, there was nothing to do but wait for word from the International Red

Cross that Luke had either been captured or killed. Days went by, however, and no word came and the hope grew that Luke had managed to escape capture and, being unable to return through the German lines, was hiding somewhere in enemy territory.

At the time of Luke's death, the 27th led every other American squadron in victories and Luke was the American Ace of Aces. Without Luke and Wehner, though, the 27th quickly fell behind Rickenbacker's 94th. Vasconcelles did get his fifth and sixth confirmed victories and Hartney achieved a certain amount of notoriety when, flying alone one night in a British Camel, he intercepted and shot down a huge, four-engined Gotha bomber. But, for the 27th Squadron, the glory days died with Wehner and Luke and there was no Distinguished Service Medal or promotion for Captain Grant.

Following the Armistice on the eleventh of November, a direct inquiry was made to the German commander in charge of prisoners of war and he certified that a Lieutenant Frank Luke was not and never had been a prisoner of the Germans. Other inquiries failed to turn up any military personnel who had knowledge of a Spad that had gone down on the evening of the 29th of September.

Then, on the tenth of December, the mayor of the town of Murvaux approached an American graves registration unit with the information that an American aviator, killed on the evening of the 29th of September, was buried in the cemetery at Murvaux. The Air Service was immediately informed and both Hartney and Vasconcelles were present when the body was disinterred the following day.

The body, clothed in the blood soaked flying suit of an American aviator, was too badly decomposed to be immediately identified. All the flyer's personal effects and identification tags had been removed from the pockets and all the insignia had been torn from the flying suit.

Because of the date of the burial and because of the light blonde hair that was clearly evident, both Hartney and Vasconcelles believed that it must be Luke. Further investigation revealed that when the Germans had stripped the body they had missed an Elgin wrist watch that was hidden under the sleeve of the flying suit. When checked with squadron records, the serial number of the watch proved to be identical to the one issued to Luke and all doubt was removed. The body was taken and reburied at the Meuse-

Argonne Military Cemetery at Romage-sous-Mountfaucon. An interrogation of several residents of Murvaux produced an account of the last minutes of Luke's life. They had seen the glow of the three balloons burning in the direction of Dun and they had heard the sound of the ground batteries just before the second and third balloons had burst into flames.

A Spad had then appeared at a low altitude over Murvaux and strafed a number of German soldiers that were in the street, killing six and wounding as many more. Then, when the Spad was less than half a kilometer past the town, the engine was heard to stop abruptly and the aircraft dropped from sight below the trees.

Several squads of troops were quickly organized and sent off down the road in the direction that the Spad had taken. A number of the town's citizens had followed at some distance behind the German soldiers. They had seen the Spad sitting upright in a meadow and they had seen the German soldiers find the cockpit empty.

After that, it had grown quite dark and they had seen nothing more, but they had heard a number of shots fired. Later, some of the French had been ordered to bring a horse and wagon out from the village and they had loaded into it the body of an American aviator and the bodies of two German soldiers.

Other residents of the village had been pressed into service to push the Spad to the edge of the meadow and to help dismantle it. They reported that the fabric on the wings and fuselage was heavily shredded, that the engine and radiator were damaged and that there was a great deal of blood in the cockpit. Early the following morning, trucks came and hauled the damaged Spad away.

When the wagon with the bodies returned to the village, the German Captain in charge pushed Luke's body out of the wagon with his boot and told the French to, 'Get rid of this piece of garbage.' Accordingly they had buried Luke in a corner of the local cemetery.

Working back toward Dun, Hartney and Vasconcelles were able to find any number of witnesses who had seen Luke burn the balloons at Dulcon and at Milly. At Dun, they first heard about the two Fokkers that Luke had shot down after flaming the first balloon. The large number of reliable witnesses who had observed this led the Flying Service to credit Luke with these two additional victories.

During this same time, two of Luke's ground crew managed to

borrow a motorcycle and side car and went looking for the wreck of the Hannoveraner that Luke had claimed the day he had left the formation. Starting at the town of Vailly they worked their way along the road to Joul until they came to a triangular shaped wood to the north of the road.

Leaving the motorcycle, they climbed up into the wood and soon found the wreck of a silver, double-tailed, two seater. The bodies had been taken away and souvenir hunters had removed the guns and the instruments and cut the crosses out of the fabric on the fuselage and wings. Still, enough of the aircraft remained for them to photograph with the camera that they had brought with them. Upon the presentation of this evidence, one more aircraft was added to Luke's score, bringing his total to 21 and making him, after Rickenbacker, the second ranking American ace.

When the details of Luke's last flight and the manner of his death had been made clear, Captain Grant submitted a formal request for Luke to be awarded the Congressional Medal of Honor. The request was quickly endorsed by Hartney and Colonel Mitchell and by General Pershing himself.

On April 14th, 1919, Frank Luke was posthumously awarded the Congressional Medal of Honor. He was the first American aviator to be so honored.

Epilogue

☆ ☆ ☆

Was Frank Luke the greatest pilot of the first World War? Or was he just an undisciplined, Arizona cowboy, with a fair amount of talent and a world of guts, riding a hot streak out to its inevitable conclusion?

On the basis of victories alone, Luke certainly ranks far down the list of aces. In fact, over one hundred flyers representing seven different countries had more than Luke's twenty one confirmed victories. Herman Goering, for example, had twenty two.

Luke's numbers become significant only when the short span of time in which they were achieved is taken into consideration. Beginning with his first confirmed victory on September 12th, Luke chalked up thirteen victories in only seven days. Only one other pilot, over the entire course of the war, ever recorded so many victories in a week's time. That pilot was the great Canadian ace, Billy Bishop, who ran his victory count from 59 to 72 during a single week in July of 1918. None of Bishop's victories however, were over the highly maneuverable and deadly Fokker D-VIIs that Luke and Wehner battled on an almost daily basis. And Bishop never made as much as a single pass at an enemy balloon.

From the twelfth of September to his death on September 29th, Luke flew a total of ten combat patrols. In every one of those patrols he succeeded in scoring at least one victory. No other pilot in the war ever ran up such a string of consecutive, successful missions. In those ten patrols, Luke had twenty confirmed victories. No other pilot in the war ever had as many as twenty victories in a month.

On September 18th and again on September 29th, Luke had five confirmed victories in a single patrol. No other pilot in the war ever had five victories in a single patrol. Rene Fonck, France's leading ace with 75 confirmed victories, twice had five victory days, but in each case, Fonck required two patrols to record those five victories.

No one who knew Luke ever doubted that he was the greatest flyer that they had ever seen. Major Hartney, who was an ace in the British Air Service before taking command of the 27th, knew most of the great British aces and never hesitated to rank Luke above any of them, even above the Canadian ace, Bill Barker, who won the Victoria Cross when he shot down four Fokkers in a single fight in October of 1918.

Rickenbacker, America's leading ace with 26 confirmed victories, was always quick to point out that, had he lived, Luke could have easily doubled any score that he could have put up.

Nungesser, who stood third on the list of French aces, knew both Fonck and Guynemer, the only two French flyers who exceeded him in victories, and he, along with all of the famous Storks, recognized that Luke's unique combination of courage and ability set him apart in a class all by himself.

Even the Germans, in their own way, acknowledged Luke's greatness by burying his body, stripped of all identification, in an unmarked grave. So humiliated were they by the repeated successes of Wehner and Luke against the best defenses that they could put up, that they could not bring themselves to provide Luke with the kind of military funeral that was customary for a pilot of his stature.

Time has dealt kindly with the memory of Frank Luke. His body rests in a place of honor in front of the main flag pole at the Meuse Argonne Military Cemetery. His statue is set in front of the State Capitol in Phoenix, Arizona. Clothed in full flying gear and carrying his helmet, he stands expectantly as if awaiting the sunrise. Eyes that cannot see, search the eastern horizon for the first signs of the coming day. Ears that cannot hear, listen for the scrape of hanger doors being opened and the ragged bark of cold engines being coaxed into life.

Having died young, this Frank Luke can never grow old. He remains forever the laughing eyed terror that set bonfire after bonfire burning across the evening sky that last September of the Great War to end all wars.